To the children of Africa,
with love from Madiba

A part of the proceeds of this book goes to
the Nelson Mandela Children's Fund

Madiba Magic

Nelson Mandela's
favourite stories for children

Tafelberg

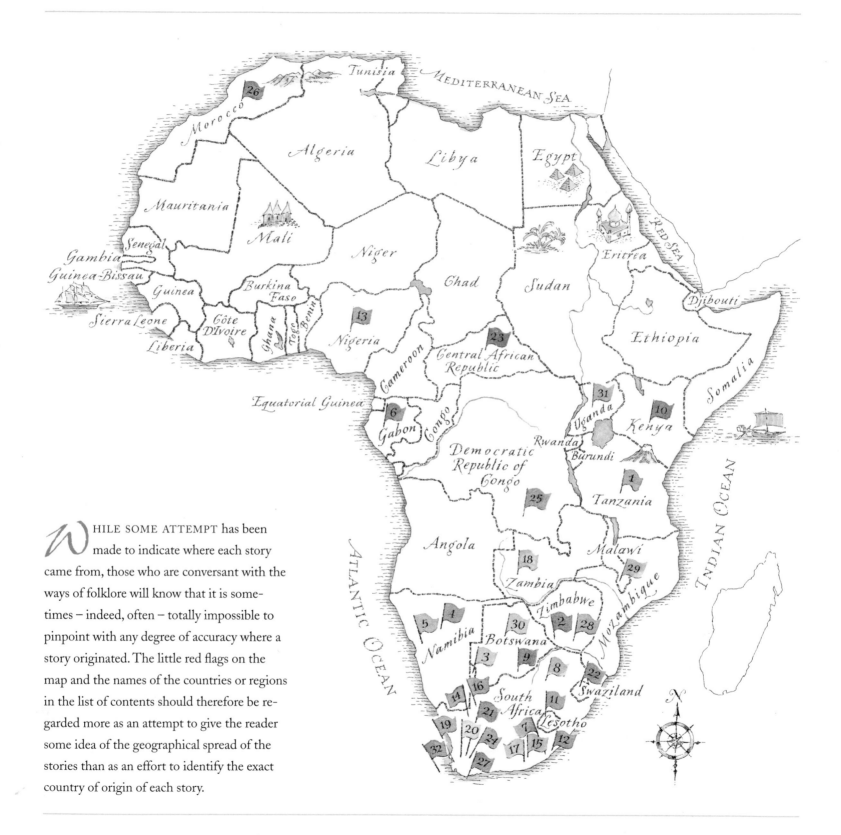

WHILE SOME ATTEMPT has been made to indicate where each story came from, those who are conversant with the ways of folklore will know that it is sometimes – indeed, often – totally impossible to pinpoint with any degree of accuracy where a story originated. The little red flags on the map and the names of the countries or regions in the list of contents should therefore be regarded more as an attempt to give the reader some idea of the geographical spread of the stories than as an effort to identify the exact country of origin of each story.

Contents

© 2002 in this selection Tafelberg Publishers Ltd,
28 Wale Street, Cape Town

Consulting editor: Linda Rode
Editor: Marguerite Gordon
Art director: Ann Walton
Designer: Teresa Williams
Cover illustration by Natalie Hinrichsen
Vignettes by Teresa Williams
Map by Abdul Amien
Set in 12 on 16 pt Caslon by Teresa Williams
Reproduction by Unifoto, Cape Town
Printed and bound by Tien Wah Press (Pte) Ltd, Singapore
First edition, third impression 2004

ISBN 0 624 04073 9

Foreword

"We do not really mean, we do not really mean,
that what we are going to say is true."

THESE ARE THE WORDS with which Ashanti story-tellers begin their stories, and perhaps they are a fitting introduction to an anthology such as this one, since the majority of the stories have undergone many metamorphoses over the centuries. They have acquired frills and tails and sometimes defected from one people or ethnic group to another.

Because a story is a story, and you may tell it as your imagination and your being and your environment dictate; and if your story grows wings and becomes the property of others, you may not hold it back. One day it will return to you, enriched by new details and with a new voice. This particular characteristic of folk tales is illustrated in the traditional conclusion of the Ashanti narrator: "This is my story which I have related, if it be sweet or if it be not sweet, take some elsewhere and let some come back to me."

In this anthology, some of the oldest African tales, after their travels for many centuries in far-flung places, are given back, with new voices, to the children of Africa. This collection offers a handful of beloved stories, morsels rich with the gritty essence of Africa, but in many instances universal in their portrayal of humanity, beasts and the mystical.

Children will discover again a variety of favourite themes in African tales, or perhaps unearth them for the first time. There is that cunning creature who manages to outsmart everyone, including much bigger opponents: Hlakanyana of the Zulu and Xhosa, and Sankhambi of the Venda; the hare, sly little rascal that he is; the cunning jackal, most often in the role of a trickster; the hyena (sometimes associated with the wolf) in the role of underdog; the lion as ruler and distributor of gifts to the animals; the snake, which inspires fear but is also a symbol of healing power, often in conjunction with the power of water; magic spells which bring either doom or freedom; people and animals undergoing metamorphoses; gruesome cannibals who terrorise both great and small.

The collection also includes some new stories from different parts of South Africa and the continent to supplement those ancient treasures.

It is my wish that the voice of the storyteller will never die in Africa, that all the children in Africa may experience the wonder of books and that they will never lose the capacity to enlarge their earthly dwelling place with the magic of stories.

Mandela

The Enchanting Song of the Magical Bird

This East African story about the innocence and power that children possess was recorded at the beginning of the twentieth century in Benaland, Tanganyika (now Tanzania), by Pastor JULIUS OELKE of the Berlin Mission Church. The illustrator is PIET GROBLER.

ONE DAY, A STRANGE BIRD arrived in a small village that nestled among low hills. From that moment on, nothing was safe. Anything the villagers planted in the fields disappeared overnight. Every morning there were fewer and fewer sheep and goats and chickens. Even during the day, while the people were working on the lands, the gigantic bird would come and break open their storehouses and granaries, and steal from them their food supplies for winter.

The villagers were devastated. There was misery in the land – everywhere was the sound of wailing and the gnashing of teeth. No one – not even the bravest hero of the village – could get his hands on the bird. It was just too quick for them. They hardly ever saw it: they just heard the rushing of its great wings as it came to perch in the crown of the old yellowwood tree, under its thick canopy of leaves.

The headman of the village tore out his hair in frustration. One day, after the bird had plundered his own livestock and winter supplies, he commanded the older men to sharpen their axes and machetes and to move as one against the bird. "Cut down the tree – that is the answer," he said.

With axes and machetes ground to gleaming razor-edges, the older men approached the great tree. The first blows landed heavily and bit deep into the flesh of the trunk. The tree shuddered, and from the thick, tangled leaves of its crown the strange and mysterious bird emerged. A honey-sweet song came from its throat. It reached into the hearts of the men and spoke of fabulous, far-off things that never would return. So enchanting was the sound that the machetes and the axes fell one by one from the hands of the men. They sank to their knees and stared upwards in longing and yearning at the bird that sang for them in all its brilliantly coloured splendour.

The men's hands became weak. Their hearts became soft. No, they thought, so beautiful a bird could never have caused such damage and destruction! And when the sun sank red in the west, they shuffled like sleepwalkers back to the headman and told him there was nothing, but nothing, that they could do to harm the bird.

The headman was very angry. "Then the young men of the tribe will have to help me," he said. "Let the youngsters break the power of the bird."

The next morning the young men took their gleaming axes and machetes and set off for the tree. The first blows again landed heavily, biting deep into the flesh of the trunk. And, just as before, the green canopy of the tree opened and the strange bird appeared in all its multihued finery. Once again a most wonderful melody echoed across the hills. The young men listened, enchanted, to the song that spoke to them of love and courage and of the heroic deeds that awaited them. This bird could not be bad, they thought. This bird could not be wicked. The young men's arms became weak, the axes and machetes fell from their hands, and they knelt like the older men before them, listening in a trance to the song of the bird.

When night fell, they stumbled, bewildered, back to the headman. In their ears still sounded the enchanting song of the mysterious bird. "It is impossible," said the leader of their group. "No one can withstand the magical power of this bird."

The headman was furious. "Only the children remain," he said. "Children hear truly and their eyes are clear. I will lead the children against the bird."

The next morning the headman and the children of the tribe went to the tree where the strange bird was resting. As soon as the children let the tree feel the bite of the axe, the leafy canopy opened and the bird appeared just as before – blindingly beautiful. But the children did not look up. Their eyes stayed on the axes and machetes in their hands. And they chopped, chopped, chopped to the rhythm of their own music.

The bird began to sing. The headman could hear that its song was beautiful beyond compare, and he could feel the weakness in his hands. But the children's ears could hear only the dull, regular sounds of their axes and machetes. And no matter how enchantingly the bird sang, the children continued to chop, chop, chop.

Eventually the trunk creaked and cracked apart. The tree crashed to the ground and with it fell the strange and mysterious bird. The headman found the bird where it lay, crushed to death by the weight of the branches.

From everywhere the people came charging. The hardened older men and the strong young men could not believe what the children with their thin arms had accomplished!

That night, the headman declared a great feast to reward the children for what they had done. "You are the only ones who hear truly and whose eyes are clear," he said. "You are the eyes and the ears of our tribe."

Translator: DARREL BRISTOW-BOVEY

The Cat Who Came Indoors

There are quite a number of stories explaining how dogs were tamed, but this Shona story from Zimbabwe, originally told to the musicologist and folklorist HUGH TRACEY in the Karanga tongue, explains how cats became cherished inhabitants of human homes. The illustration is by JEAN FULLALOVE.

ONCE UPON A TIME, there was a cat, a wild cat, who lived all by herself out in the bush. After a while she got tired of living alone and took herself a husband, another wild cat who she thought was the finest creature in all the jungle.

One day, as they strolled together along the path through the tall grass, *swish*, out of the grass jumped Leopard, and Cat's husband was bowled over, all fur and claws, into the dust.

"O-oh!" said Cat. "I see my husband is covered in dust and is not the finest creature in all the jungle. It is Leopard." So Cat went to live with Leopard.

They lived together very happily until one day, as they were hunting in the bush, suddenly – *whoosh* – out of the shadows leapt Lion right onto Leopard's back and ate him all up.

"O-o-oh!" said Cat. "I see Leopard is not the finest creature in all the jungle. It is Lion."

So Cat went to live with Lion.

They lived together very happily until one day, as they were stalking through the forest, a large shape loomed overhead, and – *fu-chu* – Elephant put one foot on top of Lion and squashed him flat.

"O-o-o-oh!" said Cat. "I see Lion is not the finest creature in all the jungle. It is Elephant."

So Cat went to live with Elephant. She climbed up onto his back and sat purring on his neck, right between his two ears.

They lived together very happily until one day, as they were moving through the tall reeds down by the river – *pa-wa!* – there was a loud bang, and Elephant sank down onto the ground.

Cat looked around and all she could see was a small man with a gun.

"O-o-o-o-oh!" said Cat. "I see Elephant is not the finest creature in all the jungle. It is Man."

So Cat walked after Man all the way to his home, and jumped up onto the thatch of his hut.

"At last," said Cat, "I have found the finest creature in all the jungle."

She lived up in the thatch of the hut very happily and began to catch the mice and rats which lived in that village. Until one day, as she sat on the roof warming herself in the sun, she heard a noise from inside the hut.

The voices of Man and his wife grew louder and louder until – *wara-wara-wara* . . . *yo-we!* – out came Man, tumbling head over heels into the dust.

"Aha!" said Cat. "Now I *do* know who is truly the finest creature in all the jungle. It is Woman."

Cat came down from the thatch, went inside the hut, and sat by the fire.

And that is where she's been ever since.

The Great Thirst

This San tale explains how the first animals found grazing and water.
It is retold here by the folklorist PIETER W. GROBBELAAR
and illustrated by JUDY WOODBORNE.

LONG, LONG AGO, when Kaggen created the animals, there were no fountains, rivers or waterholes on earth. All that they had to drink was each other's blood, and they ate the flesh off each other's bones. Yes, those were blood-red days and no one's life was safe.

Then Elephant, the great one, said, "This can't go on. I wish I were dead. Then my bones could become fruit trees and my sinews could become tendrils that spread over the ground and bear tsammas, and my hair could become a grassy field."

And the animals asked him, "How long must we still wait, Elephant? How long must we still wait? Because elephants live for a long, long time!"

"That I don't know," said Elephant. "We'll have to see."

But Snake said, "I'll help you!" And before Elephant could move, he had bitten Elephant with his poison fangs, holding on to him until Elephant died.

Then the animals stormed forward! Lion and Leopard, Jackal and Hare, and even old Tortoise with his knock-knees. They ate and ate of Elephant's flesh, and drank his blood, and stopped only when all that remained were his bones and sinews and hair. Then they went to sleep, as everyone had eaten quite enough.

But when they awoke the next day, the animals began to complain again. "Now that Elephant is dead and his flesh eaten up, where are we going to get food?" And if they had had tears, they would surely have cried, but the sun had caused their bodies to become dried up, even their eyes.

"Don't worry!" said Snake. "Remember Elephant's promise?"

"He said that when he *died* . . ." said the animals. "But you have *killed* him."

"Don't complain so," said Snake. "Let us not be hasty. Wait and see. Is there anyone who would drink *my* blood?"

But the animals were scared of his poison fangs and kept quiet.

That night, when the stars rose one by one from their resting place, there was a new fire in the sky. "It's Elephant's spirit!" said the frightened animals. "Now he is definitely coming to destroy us all."

"Wait and see," said Snake.

And Elephant's eyes were two shining, burning coals that climbed high into the sky till they stopped right over the place where the animals had devoured his body.

And suddenly his bones stood upright and they grew roots and branches full of fruit. And his sinews spread all over the earth and bore tsamma melons. And his hair became a grassy field that was a pasture.

"Now we have food!" exclaimed the animals as they began to graze. But some of the animals who couldn't survive without meat and blood crept away in the night. They were Lion and Leopard, Jackal and Wolf, Wildcat and Owl.

And when the other animals went to sleep, they came out stealthily to kill and devour. Hawk was so cheeky that he sought his prey in broad daylight. Only Vulture said, "I also want meat, but I'll not kill for it myself."

Even though they now had food, the animals were still not happy.

"Water! Water! Water!" they complained. "We're dying of thirst."

"But the fruit is full of water," said Snake. "And the tsammas and the grass."

"Water! Water! Water!" groaned the animals and, as before, they began looking amongst each other for the youngest, sweetest blood to drink.

"Elephant gave his body for you," said Snake angrily. "And I gave my poison for you. But you never stop complaining." The animals did not realise that Snake had used up all his poison to kill huge Elephant. "Wait a minute. I'll make water for you!" said Snake.

Then Snake disappeared into a hole in the ground and he hissed and blew and spewed out streams of water until the water bubbled above the ground, over the empty plains and into the low-lying areas.

"Now we have a fountain and rivers and waterholes!" said the animals, feeling very satisfied.

So that is how the animals received their food and water, and even today we hear about elephant grass and the water snake.

Translator: DIANNE STEWART

King Lion's Gifts

A Khoi narrative in which the first animals receive tails, horns and hides from King Lion, retold here by PIETER W. GROBBELAAR *and illustrated by* MARNA HATTINGH.

KING LION WAS HOSTING a huge party and every single animal had to go, because an invitation from the king was law, and one couldn't refuse it. Only the female buck dug in their heels. "Oh no," said Mrs Kudu. "Lion is only too glad to feast on members of our family. How do we know he isn't going to eat us if we go to his party?"

"Yes, yes, yes!" agreed a whole group of female buck.

"Then I'll just go alone," said Kudu. "If I don't go, there might be trouble."

"Yes, let's go," said the other male buck.

The female buck snorted angrily and didn't move a hoof. Only the old Nanny Goat couldn't resist an invitation that included food – even if the others might end up eating her!

And so the animals began to arrive. Leopard and Rabbit, and Zebra and Mole, and Elephant and Polecat and Snake. Baboon was too inquisitive to stay away;

Donkey was too stupid. Rock-rabbit and Hippopotamus and Rock-lizard were there too, and Hyena and Jackal. Oh, yes – it was the party to end all parties.

First they danced a little and Baboon took the lead. Then they sang a little and Jackal was in fine voice. After that they ate honey and drank milk. Even Lion and Leopard and Lynx and Hyena ate with the others, as though they had never tasted blood. But Lion had considered that, at a party, one could hardly serve up the guests' family members.

"Listen now, my animals!" said Lion when he had licked the honey pot clean (because a king eats first and last and quite a lot in between, too – the others just have to take what they can get). "Listen, my animals!" he said again. "I would like to give each one of you a gift to show you what a good king I am."

"Thank you, thank you, thank you!" cried the animals, and they jockeyed for position, each one afraid that the other would get the best present before he could get to the front.

"Steady on!" roared Lion. "Anyone who grabs will get nothing – and the greedy will get last."

That settled things down a bit.

"Those of you who would like horns," said Lion, "stand to one side!"

"Horns?" Kudu asked his friends. "Don't you think we would look good with horns?"

"Yes, yes, yes," cried the buck, and stood to one side.

"Here," said Lion, and they put the horns on. "But the female buck who stayed away get nothing."

Elephant saw the buck parading and he threw his hefty weight around to get close to Lion. "I also want horns," he said and grabbed a pair of pretty white ones with his mouth.

"Greedy-guts!" growled Lion. "Because you were so greedy, the horns will stay stuck in your mouth, and you won't be able to carry them high on your head, like the buck."

"Oh my goodness!" gasped Elephant. "Now my nose is too short. I can't . . . I can't . . . I can't . . . breathe!"

"Take that!" said Lion, and he pulled Elephant by his nose till it was almost dragging on the ground. "Is that better?"

"Thank you," mumbled Elephant, and he shuffled away with his horn teeth and his dangling nose.

But there was already another to-do on the heap of horns. It was Rhinoceros who was poking around.

"Oh, well," said Lion, "since you want to poke your nose in everywhere, your horns will stick to your nose."

"Oh, no – I won't take any of that!" said Rhinoceros, and he promptly tried to attack his king with the horns on his nose. But Lion gave him such a smack that he

lost the tip of one of his horns and his eyes were nearly swollen shut. That's why, to this day, Rhinoceros still sees so badly and has an odd pair of horns.

Lion walked over to the next heap. "Here are beautiful ears!" he said.

Well, animals are just like children: they don't have ears, and they don't want any either. But Lion was already holding two pairs of long ears, and he refused to put down what he had already picked up, because he was the king. "Oh, take these, then!" he said, and put them on the first two animals within reach. They were Donkey and Rabbit. And they just had to say thank you.

"Those who want nice clothes!" called Lion.

Now that caused consternation. Lion really had to keep his wits about him, because the animals were quite keen to show off. Each wanted to look better than his neighbour.

Leopard got a spotted suit. Zebra was dressed in a striped jacket. But Horse and Cow had a long story.

"We work on the farm," said Horse.

"And we have to dress neatly every day," said Cow.

"One suit of clothes is not enough," said Horse.

"We surely don't want the farmer to laugh at us animals," said Cow.

"All right, all right," said Lion, because he liked Horse's swagger and Cow had such a gentle voice that it turned even a king's heart soft. "Come here!"

Horse was first. Oh, but pretty is hardly the word! Horse got suits that were dapple-grey and chestnut, dark brown and snow-white, and black as the dead of night itself. "Thank you very much," said Horse, and he cantered away. But after a while he got tired of all the dressing and undressing, and he divided the clothes among his children. And that's why, even today, each horse has only one suit of clothes but every horse looks different.

Cow got a multicoloured dress and a red jacket and black Sunday best. But later she did as Horse had done and gave them to her children.

While Lion was still busy with Cow, a voice from the crowd shrieked, "Hey, what about me? Don't give all the best to Horse and Cow!" It was Giraffe.

"How rude!" exclaimed Lion. "How dare you shout at your king? Now you will never speak again!" And so it came about that Giraffe lost his voice.

Just to show the animals that he would not be hurried, Lion took a stroll to the heap of horns again and chose a couple for Cow, to match every outfit he had given her.

"Thank you very much," said Cow, and she walked away with her gifts.

But Giraffe looked so forlorn, even though he couldn't say a word, that Lion felt sorry for him. "Here's a really special suit for you," said the king, "and a pair of horns to go with it."

Giraffe put on his suit and his horns and already he looked better. Lion looked him up and down. "And I will give you a long neck so that you can see your enemies from a long way off," he said. "And long legs so that you can run away quickly." Then Giraffe was delighted, and he trotted away satisfied.

Just as Lion wanted to turn around again, something moved between his paws. "Hey!" he shouted and jumped into the air, and before the culprit could get away, Lion had squashed him underfoot. It was Rock-

lizard, who crept out from between Lion's claws with his head bruised black and blue. "It's your own fault," said the king. "Now you will always have a blue head."

Lion was starting to get impatient, because the sun was sinking low and his stomach was starting to rumble. Milk and honey aren't really food fit for the king of the beasts.

So then the animals just had to take what they could get. Baboon got a tail like a sickle. Rock-rabbit and Mole each got a long, thin one but they didn't want them and quietly went to bury them. Then they had nothing.

Goat got a beard and before Nanny Goat knew what was happening, she had one too. The animals chuckled to themselves, but King Lion pressed on. "Next! Next!" he called.

Hippopotamus was saddled with four giant teeth, and Snake accidentally got Lion's own calabash of herb medicine which he had stolen from a hunter. Snake knocked back the brew in one gulp. It started to ferment, and Snake just wanted to spit; it turned into poison and he just wanted to bite.

"Cut off his legs!" cried King Lion. But it didn't help. Snake was so crazed by that stage that he just slithered away on his stomach, and even today he bites whatever he sees, and his poison is more dangerous than ever.

Polecat, on the other hand, got hold of Mrs Lion's little jar of perfume and poured the entire contents all over himself. Gracious, it was quite a smell! The animals held their noses and grabbed whatever they could: horns, hooves and wagging tails. And then they scuttled away.

"What about us?" whined Hyena and Jackal, who still didn't have anything because they were too fussy.

Tired of all the effort, Lion looked around, but there

were only a wail and a laugh left over. "Take what you want," he said, "and don't hang around for a minute longer!"

The two had to grab what was there. And that is why, even today, Hyena still has the loudest laugh of all the animals and there is no beast who can out-wail Jackal.

When old Tortoise finally got to the place where the gifts had been handed out, there was not an animal or gift in sight. That is why he still trundles around in the horny shell that Crocodile made for him. And Frog lives quite naked in the water. All the waiting had made him so hot that he had gone for a quick swim, but someone stole his clothes. Now he is too shy to appear in front of the other animals. If he is sunning himself a little and he hears something move, he immediately dives into the water. But at night, when it is dark, he and his brothers come out and then you can hear them complaining.

"Where? Where? Where?" complains one. "Clothing! Clothing! Clothing!" complain the others.

Translator: MARGUERITE GORDON

The Message

A Nama variation on the theme of how death came into the world, retold here by poet, novelist and short-story writer GEORGE WEIDEMAN, who heard it from Grandma Rachel Eises. In the countless versions of this ancient tale the message is sometimes brought by the chameleon and the lizard, while sometimes the hare bungles the message all by himself. In this variation Tick and Hare are the messengers. Illustrator: ROBERT HICHENS.

THIS IS THE STORY of Full Moon, Tick and Hare, and the message that Moon sent to the people a long, long time ago.

This was no ordinary message! Indeed, it was a most important message. Because, you see, Moon does not really die. She comes back again, as we see each time at full moon. And Moon wanted the people to know this truth: "Just as I die and come alive again, so you also shall die and live again."

Moon decided that Tick should be the one to take this important message to the people. She knew that lazy Tick would just sit in the shade of a shrub and wait for a goat or a goatherd to come past. Then he would jump onto one of them and hitch a ride to the kraal where the fires were, and the message would reach the people in no time at all. So Tick was given the message to pass on.

But unfortunately, Tick was not only lazy – he did not see very well either. When Tick departed from Moon with the message, it was still night. He crept under the nearest tuft of grass and slept until the goats started grazing. There he awaited his opportunity.

As the first shadow fell across the tuft of grass, Tick crept out, crawled up the shinbone in front of him and held on tight. But, ohhh . . . Tick had made a terrible mistake. As he kept repeating the message over and over to himself, so as not to forget it, the earth disappeared from underneath him, and the tkau trees and the milk bushes grew smaller and smaller.

Only then did he realise that this goat had feathers instead of fur! The sandgrouse squawked as she prepared to land on a far-away bush. She shook her feathers vigorously, and Tick flew through the air and landed on a tuft of reeds.

That same evening Moon peeped through the milk bushes on the far side, hoping to see the people dancing for joy at hearing the good news. But it was very quiet

and the fires were burning low. From the weeping of the children, she could hear that someone was very ill. Then Moon realised that Tick had not yet delivered the good news to the people.

That night a few drops of rain fell, so on the second day the sand around Tick was humming with springbok and gemsbok gambolling for joy. A shadow fell across the tuft of reeds where Tick sat waiting and Tick thought, "This is it," and he clambered on.

Oh no, but this was not a goat to whose shinbone Tick was attached! By the time Tick realised this, the gemsbok was already galloping past the kraal, along the trail of raindrops yonder, in the direction of the sunset.

When the gemsbok stopped to graze in the late afternoon, Tick realised that another day had gone by without the message having been delivered. And now the kraal lay beyond the ridge that was beyond the furthest ridge still.

A while later, when Moon peeped through the milk bushes, she saw that the fires were even smaller than on the previous evening and she heard the people wailing. Someone was very, very ill indeed, and Moon realised that Tick had still not delivered her message of joy to the people.

On the third day, while Tick was sitting on a sorrel plant, Hare came to nibble the juicy leaves. And Tick told him about his problem.

Hare, who was terribly inquisitive, immediately wanted to know what the message was, and Tick rattled it off: "Just as I, Moon, die but come alive again, so shall you also die and live again."

"This is an important message," thought Hare to himself. "If I can deliver it to the people, I shall be in favour with Moon." At once he offered to take Tick to the kraal.

They had hardly reached the nearest milk bushes when Hare gave his kaross, his furry blanket, a good shake – and Tick flew through the air. In the blink of an eye, Hare called, "Out of my way!" and hot-tailed it to the kraal, to deliver the message to the people.

However, whereas Tick was near-sighted, Hare was short-sighted. All he thought about was the fame and fortune he would receive for delivering the important message. He did not keep repeating it to himself, as Tick had; he hot-footed it so that his ears and his fluffy white tail just glanced over the pebbles and the tufts of grass.

But when he arrived at the kraal, all out of breath, Hare could not quite remember the message as Tick had told it to him. He kept repeating it, but the more he repeated it, the more the words were scrambled and the more confused he became.

Dusty and pale, he collapsed on the ground and delivered the following message to the people: "Just as I die, and remain dead, so shall you die and perish." All the people of the kraal began wailing and covering themselves in sand and ash, and at that very moment, the very, very, very sick man breathed his last.

That night, when Moon peeped through the milk bushes, she did not see a single live coal. The kraal was deserted. The people had all left. There was no sign of life.

When she looked closely, she could not see Tick anywhere, but Hare was still at the fireplace, repeating the scrambled message in a daze.

Moon was furious. She grabbed a log of burnt-out wood and hit Hare across the face with it. Hare took such fright that he dropped his kaross into the ashes of the fireplace. Then he snatched it back and hit Moon in the face with it.

Since that day, Hare has had a cleft palate, and the pale ash-dust is still visible on Moon's face.

Translator: LEILA LATIMER

The Snake Chief

The folklorist DIANA PITCHER grew up in Zululand and heard this story from her nanny, Miriam Majola, a wonderful storyteller. Later she found that the theme of a young girl who breaks a curse through her steadfastness often appears on the West Coast of Africa. The snake in a mystical role is an equally popular motif in African tales. In this retelling the story has been set in Zululand. Illustration: BABA AFRIKA.

NANDI WAS VERY POOR. Her husband was dead and she had no sons to herd cattle and only one daughter to help in the fields.

In summer, when the umdoni trees were full of creamy flowers, she and her daughter dug for ama-dumbe to eat with their maize porridge. But in autumn, when the flowers had died, she collected the umdoni berries, purple and sweet, and gave them to her neighbours in return for strips of dried goat meat or calabashes of thick and creamy sour milk.

One hot day Nandi went down to the river as usual to gather the purple berries, but nothing could she find. Not a single berry was to be seen – not one.

Just then she heard a loud hissing, a loud and terrible hissing. Looking up, she saw a great green-grey snake wound round and round the dark red trunk of the tree, his head swaying among the branches. He was eating all the berries.

"You are stealing my berries," she called. "Oh, Snake, you are stealing all my berries. What will I have to exchange for meat if you take all the fruit?"

Snake hissed again and started to slither down the trunk. Nandi was afraid, but if she ran away there would be no berries for her.

"What will you give me in exchange for the umdoni berries?" he hissed. "If I fill your basket, will you give me your daughter?"

"Yes," cried Nandi, "I'll give you my daughter this very night. Only let me fill my basket with the purple fruit."

But once her basket was full and Nandi was on her way home she began to tremble at what she had promised. How could she give her daughter to such an ugly creature? She must make sure that Snake did not find out where she lived. She must not go straight home lest he were watching.

She crossed the river where the water ran shallow over the rocks and made her way into the bush on the other bank, silently slipping between the thorn trees. She did not know that a long thorn had scratched her leather skirt and that a tiny piece of leather was left caught on a tree.

She made her way carefully and silently through the reeds, keeping an eye open for Crocodile, and waded through the deep pool. She did not know that a plump, purple berry had fallen from her basket and was floating behind her in the water.

She crept towards a huge ant-hill. Once she was behind that, she could not possibly be seen from the umdoni trees. But she caught her foot in the entrance to Water-rat's secret tunnel. She did not know that she left three beads from her anklet lying in the soft brown earth.

At last she reached her hut and cried out to her daughter, "My child, I have done an evil deed. I have promised you to Snake in return for this basket of purple fruit." And she burst into tears.

Meanwhile Snake had slithered down the tree to follow Nandi. This way and that his head swayed, until he saw the little piece of leather on the thorn and he knew which way to go.

This way and that his head swayed again, until he saw a ripe, purple berry floating in the deep pool and he knew which way to go.

This way and that his head swayed once more, until he saw three beads lying at the mouth of Water-rat's tunnel and he knew which way to go.

Just as Nandi burst into tears, there was a loud hissing at the entrance to her hut and Snake slid in, coiling his long green-grey body.

"No! No!" cried Nandi. "I did not mean my promise. I cannot give you my daughter."

The young girl looked up. Her dark brown eyes were gentle and quite fearless.

"A promise is a promise, Mother," she said. "You must surely give me to Snake." She put out her hand and stroked his green-grey head. "Come," she said, "I will find you some food." And she fetched a calabash full of thick and creamy sour milk for him to drink. Then she folded her blanket and made a bed for her snake master.

During the night Nandi stirred. What had wakened her? Had Leopard coughed? Had Hyena sung to the moon? Something had disturbed her. She listened again. Voices. She could hear voices. That was her daughter speaking. But whose was that other voice? That deep, strong voice?

Silently she crept from her skin blankets. What did she see? Was she still asleep and dreaming? Sitting with her daughter was a handsome young man, tall, brown and strong. Surely a chief's son, perhaps even a chief. Her daughter was making a bead necklace, weaving a wedding pattern with the multicoloured beads. And the young man was talking gently and lovingly to her as she worked.

Nandi looked at the folded blanket where Snake had been put to rest. On it lay a long, coiled, green-grey skin. She snatched it up and flung it into the fire that still burned low in the middle of the hut.

"Now is the spell broken," spoke the snake chief. "For a virtuous girl took pity on me and a foolish old woman has burned my skin." But in spite of his harsh words he smiled gently at Nandi.

Nandi now has three grandchildren – a boy to herd the cattle on the veld and two girls to help her hoe the weeds from among the maize plants and to dig for amadumbe. She no longer needs to gather umdoni berries, for there is enough food for all.

How Hlakanyana Outwitted the Monster

The trickster Hlakanyana is one of the most important mythical figures in Zulu folklore. But characters similar to Hlakanyana are also found in the stories of other indigenous language groups. For this retelling JACK COPE, who had grown up hearing these stories being told around the evening fires in Zululand, drew on the oldest recorded accounts of Nguni folklore. Illustration: NEELS BRITZ.

HLAKANYANA HAD LEFT his mother and run away from home because the warriors were hunting for him. He walked along on his journey over the earth, but he had nothing to make music with and nothing happy to sing about. He was very tired and very hungry.

On a small hill from where he could see for a long distance in all directions, Hlakanyana came upon a hare which had its lair in the tall grass.

Hare is clever and a quick runner. Hlakanyana could not creep up on him unseen and he could never hope to catch him. So he greeted him and sat down on a stone to talk.

"Why is it you have such long ears?" he asked.

"So I can hear things even before they happen."

"Can you hear a flute playing?"

Hare listened and said he could hear no such thing.

"When I came from the river I saw the buffaloes sleeping in the shade. Now they are coming this way. If we do not run, they will trample us. I can hear them coming," Hlakanyana said.

Hare listened. "I cannot hear them," he said.

"But they are galloping this way! Clean your ears and listen again."

Hare cleaned his ears with a grass stalk and again he listened, but he could not hear the buffaloes.

"There is no time to lose!" Hlakanyana said. "Put your ears to the ground and surely you will hear the rumble of their hooves."

Hare bent his head to the ground and flattened out his long ears, and as he did so Hlakanyana jumped on his ears and pinned him down.

Hare was caught. He struggled but he could not escape. He was tasty game and Hlakanyana made short work of him, lighting a fire to roast his meal. Afterwards he kept one of Hare's hollow leg-bones and shaped it into a flute. He went along playing on his flute this song:

I met the hare.
No one is more cute.
Now he does not care –
His shinbone is a flute.

Hlakanyana came to a part of the river where there was a deep pool. Near the pool was a tree and a leguan was resting in its branches.

"Where do you come from?" asked Leguan.

Hlakanyana played on his flute and sang:

I tricked the cannibal's mother.
We played at cooking each other.
I did not burn –
She was done to a turn.

Leguan asked Hlakanyana to give him the flute. But Hlakanyana refused.

"Then I will come down and take it from you," Leguan said. He was insolent because he was close to the deep pool. He could easily dive into it and no one could follow him there.

"Come down and take the flute if you can," Hlakanyana said.

So Leguan climbed out of the tree. He has a long, heavy tail and its thin end is like the thong of a cattle whip. Hlakanyana did not know to what use Leguan could put it.

"Give me the flute and we need not fight about it," Leguan said.

"Do you think you can beat me with words because you have a double tongue?" Hlakanyana asked.

Suddenly Leguan struck with his long tail. The blow knocked Hlakanyana off his feet, he fell and the flute rolled away. Leguan picked it up and he dived into the water and disappeared from sight in the deep pool.

In this way it happened that Hlakanyana was caught unawares and lost his flute. He went on, but his heart was sore now that he had no music. He could not get the flute back. When he stopped to listen, he heard Leguan somewhere near the deep pool playing on it. He was playing a song to call the cows closer to the river so he could tie their hind legs with his tail and milk them.

Hlakanyana did not stop walking for a long time. The sun was already setting and still he had met no one along the path to guide him. At last he saw a very strange apparition sitting under a tree. It was a monster, for it had only one leg and one arm. There was only one side to its body and it had half a face, one eye and long teeth on that side of its mouth. Grass grew out of its other side.

Hlakanyana was afraid. He wanted to run away. But he saw that the monster was eating a big loaf of steamed bread which it held in its one hand. The tantalising smell of the bread made Hlakanyana's mouth water. The monster was tearing chunks off the loaf with its teeth.

"What do you want? Go away or I will tear you up and eat you too," the monster hissed. The wind of its breath when it spoke sounded like whistling in the grass.

"I am going. Why should you eat me? I have done you no wrong," Hlakanyana answered. He walked on along the path. He came to some bushes and hid behind them to watch the monster. The monster stopped eating and soon it lay down on its side like one who wants to sleep.

Hlakanyana waited a while. Then he crept back, *shi-shi-shi*. The monster was fast asleep; its snores blew in and out of the grass at the side of its head.

Hlakanyana could see the bulging bag beside the monster. "There must be another loaf of steamed bread in the bag," he thought. He crept closer, his knees knocking together.

Without making a sound Hlakanyana opened the bag, put his hand in and took out a loaf of bread even larger than the one the monster had eaten.

Just then the butcher-bird in the tree began to cry out: "Who do I kill? Who do I kill? Who do I kill? The thieves are stealing your red ox!"

The monster woke up and saw Hlakanyana running away with the loaf of bread. At once it jumped to its one foot and began to chase him.

"Stop! I will singe your hair! I will roast you on a spit!" it shouted.

It came after Hlakanyana, hopping on one long leg. Even with only one leg it moved quickly! The wind whistled through the grass growing from its other side as it ran.

Hlakanyana ran so fast that he nearly fell over his own feet. His heels were kicking against his own buttocks.

The monster gained on Hlakanyana. It reached out a hand to snatch him. *Ndi-ndi-ndi* the foot stomped as it hopped.

Under some trees, Hlakanyana saw the opening of a snake's hole. He dived down the hole with the loaf of bread and crawled in until he could go no farther. There he was stuck.

The monster had a long leg, and its arm was just as long. It thrust its hand down the hole, deeper and deeper, groping around until at last it caught Hlakanyana by the ankle.

"Ha, ha, ha! Pull away, you ugly thing; you have caught hold of the root of a tree!" Hlakanyana shouted.

The monster heard him. It did not mean to waste its strength pulling at the root of a tree. So it let go of Hlakanyana's leg and felt around with its hand down in the snake's hole. It caught hold of a strong tree root.

"Wa! We! Maye!" Hlakanyana screamed. "Let me go! You are killing me, you cannibal!"

The monster held on. It pulled and pulled. It wrenched this way and that on the root. The sweat fell in drops off the point of its half chin.

"Oh, my father! I am being torn apart!" Hlakanyana cried. "Have mercy on me – I will give you back your bread!"

The monster went on pulling at the root for a long time, until it grew tired and its fingers could no longer grip the root. It gave up the struggle and went away.

Then Hlakanyana came out of the snake's hole. He sat on a stone and ate until his stomach was full. When he had finished, he took up his stick and went on his way.

Words As Sweet As Honey from Sankhambi

Sankhambi plays a prominent role in many Venda tales – he is the equivalent of Hlakanyana in the previous story. Sometimes he is quite small, like a tortoise; sometimes big and strong. All are on their guard against him, however, for wherever Sankhambi is, trouble is brewing. This retelling by children's book specialist LINDA RODE is illustrated by VÉRONIQUE TADJO.

IN THE EARLY DAYS the monkeys were not as thin and nimble as they are today. They were furry little pot-bellied animals that moved slowly. It was such fun for the rascally Sankhambi to creep up behind them and yank their long tails. This made the monkeys furious, and from high up in the trees they would bombard him with seeds and bits of branches as he lay on his back basking in the sun.

Sankhambi did not like this monkey business one bit, and one day he decided to do something about it.

"Dear friends," he said in a sweet voice and with a twinkle in his wicked eyes, "I want to tell you a big secret."

"Don't you believe him; it's another wicked trick," warned the eldest monkey, but Sankhambi begged and pleaded with the monkeys to hear him out about this very special secret. And because monkeys are naturally curious animals, they clambered slowly down the tree trunks and drew closer, step by monkey step.

"I would like a chance to do you a favour," said Sankhambi, his voice as sweet as honey. "Up there on the mountain, next to the great lake, is a cave. And deep inside the cave is an enormous beehive full of golden honeycomb – and I am the only one who knows about it. Follow me – I will show you the way."

The monkeys eagerly fell in line behind him, thinking only of the golden delight that was waiting for them.

Eventually Sankhambi led them along a ledge to the mouth of a cave with an overhanging roof. "Go inside, friends," he offered generously.

But just as soon as the monkeys were inside, Sankhambi started to stamp his feet hard so that dull thuds echoed all around the cave.

"Oh, marula pips and beer calabashes!" he screamed, pretending to be terrified. "Friends, the roof is starting to collapse. Stretch your arms up high and hold up the

roof. I will run to fetch some poles so that we can support it. Stand still just where you are, don't move a muscle, and hold tight!"

The monkeys did exactly this: they stood dead still, with their arms stretched up above their heads to stop the roof from caving in. They stood. And they stood. Because they dared not move, otherwise the roof of the cave would collapse on their very own heads.

Oh, if only Sankhambi would come quickly with the supports!

But of course, by this time Sankhambi was trotting along down at the lake. "What a bunch of monkeys!" he hooted and went to curl up in a spot of sunlight for an undisturbed afternoon snooze.

All through the midday heat, and right through the cool of the night, as the stars lay white in the water of the great lake, there stood the monkeys like stone pillars holding up the roof of the cave with all their might.

It was only as the morning light began to glimmer in the east that the eldest monkey suddenly had a thought. He gingerly took one finger away, then another, then his whole hand, then the other hand . . . He looked at the sweating faces of his family next to him and realised Sankhambi had made fools of them all!

One by one the monkeys lowered their stiff, aching arms. And when they looked down at their bodies, they saw that their pot-belly figures had changed completely. After all the toil and sweat and stretching to hold up the roof of the cave, their bodies had become tall and slender.

And that is why, even today, monkeys are able to romp through the trees so swiftly.

Translator: MARGARET AUERBACH

Mmutla and Phiri

This hare-and-hyena tale from Botswana was told to folklorist PHYLLIS SAVORY *by Ellen Molokela. The illustration is by* JONATHAN COMERFORD.

IN THE DAYS WHEN ANIMALS conversed one with another, there were among the dwellers in the Great Thirstland of the Kalahari two medicine men, Phiri the Hyena and Mmutla the Hare.

They were on apparently friendly terms with each other, but there was a great deal of professional rivalry between them. They often had long and heated debates, each endeavouring to prove to the other his superior skill and knowledge.

"I, as the elder, am naturally endowed with more brains," snapped the hyena during one of these discussions.

"Not so," argued the hare. "It is skill and endurance that count. For instance, who of us makes the better medicine to ward off the fire's heat for the longest time?"

"You ask a foolish question," replied the hyena, "for do not all the creatures of the wilds come to me for special fire medicine when the dryness of the winter grass brings danger from this most greatly feared of all the elements?"

"Well, let us test our abilities," said the hare with cunning finality. "Let us dig a pit, and at the bottom we can each hollow out a hiding place for our own protection. Then we'll build a fire at the bottom of the hole, and each in turn shall spend a night in his prepared retreat. There we shall test our fire medicine. The one who is able to remain without harm throughout the night must surely possess the greater power."

"A capital idea!" agreed the hyena.

So they set to work and dug a deep pit. Then each made a hiding place for himself, according to the custom of his kind, in which to endure the heat of the flames.

The hyena, following his lifelong habit, dug a shallow cave, while the hare, as is the custom of his kind, began to burrow and made a warren with many tunnels.

When satisfied with his labour, each collected a large

pile of wood and took it to the bottom of the hole, where he laid it in preparation for a fire.

The hare then said, "You, Phiri, as you have mentioned, are the elder. Therefore I, being the least important, should go down first."

They climbed into the pit and the hare sat at the entrance to his tunnel, while the hyena lit the bonfire before jumping back onto the rim of the excavation to watch events unfold.

Now, the entrance to the hare's tunnel was low, and as soon as he was hidden by the smoke, Mmutla disappeared into the depths of his burrow, where the heat and the fumes could not reach him.

Presently he rushed back to the opening and called out in apparent panic, "Phiri, I am burning!"

"Stand on your head," answered the hyena.

"Phiri, I am still burning!" the hare shouted back after another dash to the opening.

"Then sit down," advised the hyena.

"Phiri, I am still burning!" shrieked the hare in apparent agony.

"Try standing up," suggested the hyena.

"Phiri, standing up is worse than sitting down – I am still burning!" Mmutla moaned, although actually holding his paw to his mouth to smother his laughter.

"Then lie down on your side," said the hyena with finality.

There followed a long silence. When the fire had died down, the hyena looked down into the pit. There was no sign of the hare. The hyena giggled to himself. Mmutla had surely been burnt to death. So he went home delighted to think that he no longer had a professional rival.

The following morning, when Phiri went to the pit to clear away the ashes, he was surprised to find Mmutla

sitting at the entrance to his tunnel, grinning broadly and apparently none the worse for his experience.

"Well," grinned the hare, "I had a pretty warm time down here to begin with, but my fire medicine could not have worked better. Come, Phiri, now it is your turn."

They laid wood at the bottom of the hyena's hole for another big fire. After the wood had been arranged to the hare's satisfaction, the hyena went into his shallow cave to test *his* fire medicine.

As soon as Phiri had settled himself comfortably in his dug-out, the hare set the wood alight. Then he climbed back to the rim of the pit to watch events.

Very soon the hyena called out, "Mmutla, I am burning!"

"Stand on your head," answered the hare.

"Mmutla, I am still burning!" shouted the hyena in great discomfort.

"Then sit down," advised the hare.

"Mmutla, I am still burning!" screamed the hyena.

"Try standing up," giggled the hare.

"Mmutla, it is worse standing up than sitting down!" moaned the hyena.

"Well, do as I did – lie down on your side!" the hare replied, and he clapped his paws for joy at the agonised moans of his rival.

There followed a loud scream, and then silence – and Mmutla went home delighted at the success of his ruse.

When he returned on the following morning, Mmutla found the charred body of the hyena lying in the shallow cave that he had dug for himself.

Gleefully he cut off one of Phiri's ears and made it into a whistle. Up and down the hare strutted, blowing a gay tune on his newly made toy, and all the animals gathered to listen to his music.

When he considered that the audience was large enough, he turned to them and sang boastingly:

I, Mmutla, am the greatest medicine man on earth;
Phiri, my rival, was but a small child.
Listen while I make music through the hole in his ear!

As he swaggered up and down, boasting of his superiority over the hyena, Tladi, the pitch-black lightning-bird who shone like the sun, flew down from the clouds overhead.

"I like your music, Mmutla," he said. "Lend me your whistle that I too may make such joyful sounds."

"What! Lend you my whistle?" laughed the hare. "Not I! You would surely fly back to the clouds with it, and how could I follow you up there?"

But Tladi was persistent in his pleading and promised the hare most faithfully that he would stay at his side while he made music on the wonderful toy.

"Very well," agreed Mmutla grudgingly, after due consideration, and he handed the whistle to Tladi.

Immediately the lightning-bird broke his word and darted straight up into the heavens, blowing a tune as he went. It soon became apparent that he had no intention whatsoever of returning the whistle to its rightful owner.

Mmutla was very angry, especially when he heard titters of laughter from among the many onlookers who had listened to his boasting. He wandered about despondently for some time, not knowing how to set about recovering his whistle. Finally he decided to ask Sekgogo the spider for advice.

"I can weave a bag around you," said Sekgogo in answer to the hare's request for help, "and pull you up to Tladi."

Without delay he began to weave a strong, thin thread round and round Mmutla until he was securely encased in a silken bag. Then Sekgogo allowed the breeze to waft him up into the sky, spinning out his thread as he rose. There he alighted on a cloud, and pulled Mmutla up after him.

As Tladi looked down from his home in the heavens, he saw Mmutla flying up towards him and he watched in growing astonishment as the hare stepped onto the cloud beside the spider.

"What?!" he exclaimed with awe. "Has Mmutla learnt to fly as well as I can? I must give him back his whistle, for he is too clever for me!" He duly handed the whistle back to its owner, and down, down, down the spider slowly lowered the hare until he was once more on the ground.

Fortunately for the hare, the silken thread was as invisible to the eyes of those below as it had been to Tladi, so the animals too thought that Mmutla had been flying, and they marvelled at his magic.

"As you have seen, my friends," said Mmutla, bowing to the crowd who had laughed at him such a short while before, "even Tladi, the magical bird of lightning, is not a match for me. Surely none can pit his skill against mine!"

Mmutla was deeply indebted to Sekgogo for his kindness in the recovery of his whistle, and it was the beginning of a friendship between the hare and the spider that has lasted through the ages.

The Lion, the Hare, and the Hyena

In this story from Kenya, told to PHYLLIS SAVORY by
Gwido Mariko, the hare and the hyena again try, as they so often do,
to outwit each other. The illustrator is TAMSIN HINRICHSEN.

A LION NAMED SIMBA once lived alone in a cave. In his younger days the solitude had not worried him, but not very long before this tale begins he had hurt his leg so badly that he was unable to provide food for himself. Eventually he began to realise that companionship had its advantages.

Things would have gone very badly for him, had not Sunguru the Hare happened to be passing his cave one day. Looking inside, Sunguru realised that the lion was starving. At once he set about caring for his sick friend and seeing to his comfort.

Under the hare's careful nursing, Simba gradually regained his strength until finally he was well enough to catch small game for the two of them to eat. Soon quite a large pile of bones began to accumulate outside the entrance to the lion's cave.

One day Nyangau the Hyena, while sniffing around in the hope of scrounging something for his supper, caught the appetising smell of marrow bones. His nose led him to Simba's cave, but as the bones could be seen clearly from inside he could not steal them with safety. Being a cowardly fellow, like the rest of his kind, he decided that the only way to gain possession of the tasty morsels would be to make friends with Simba. He therefore crept up to the entrance of the cave and gave a cough.

"Who makes the evening hideous with his dreadful croakings?" demanded the lion, rising to his feet and preparing to investigate the noise.

"It is I, your friend, Nyangau," faltered the hyena, losing what little courage he possessed. "I have come to tell you how sadly you have been missed by the animals, and how greatly we are looking forward to your early return to good health!"

"Well, get out," growled the lion, "for it seems to me that a friend would have enquired about my health long

before this, instead of waiting until I could be of use to him once more. Get out, I say!"

The hyena shuffled off with alacrity, his scruffy tail tucked between his bandy legs, followed by the insulting giggles of the hare. But he could not forget the pile of tempting bones outside the entrance to the lion's cave.

"I shall try again," resolved the thick-skinned hyena. A few days later he made a point of paying his visit while the hare was away fetching water to cook the evening meal.

He found the lion dozing at the entrance to his cave.

"Friend," simpered Nyangau, "I am led to believe that the wound on your leg is making poor progress, due to the underhand treatment that you are receiving from your so-called friend Sunguru."

"What do you mean?" snarled the lion malevolently. "I have to thank Sunguru that I did not starve to death during the worst of my illness, while you and your companions were conspicuous by your absence!"

"Nevertheless, what I have told you is true," confided the hyena. "It is well known throughout the countryside that Sunguru is purposely giving you the wrong treatment for your wound to prevent your recovery. For when you are well, he will lose his position as your housekeeper – a very comfortable living for him, to be sure! Let me warn you, good friend, that Sunguru is not acting in your best interests!"

At that moment the hare returned from the river, his gourd filled with water. "Well," he said, addressing the hyena as he put down his load, "I did not expect to see you here after your hasty and inglorious departure from our presence the other day. Tell me, what do you want this time?"

Simba turned to the hare. "I have been listening," he said, "to Nyangau's tales about you. He tells me that you are renowned throughout the countryside for your skill and cunning as a doctor. He also tells me that the medicines you prescribe are without rival. But he insists that you could have cured the wound on my leg a long time ago, had it been in your interest to do so. Is this true?"

Sunguru thought for a moment. He knew that he had to treat this situation with care, for he had a strong suspicion that Nyangau was trying to trick him.

"Well," he answered with hesitation, "yes, and no. You see, I am only a very small animal, and sometimes the medicines that I require are very big, and I am unable to procure them – as, for instance, in your case, good Simba."

"What do you mean?" spluttered the lion, sitting up and at once showing interest.

"Just this," replied the hare. "I need a piece of skin from the back of a full-grown hyena to place on your wound before it will be completely healed."

Hearing this, the lion sprang onto Nyangau before the surprised creature had time to get away. He tore a strip of skin off the foolish fellow's back from his head to his tail and clapped it on the wound on his leg. As the skin came away from the hyena's back, the hairs that remained stretched and stood on end. To this day Nyangau and his kind still have long, coarse hairs standing up on the crests of their misshapen bodies.

Sunguru's fame as a doctor spread far and wide after this episode, for the wound on Simba's leg healed without further trouble. But it was many weeks before the hyena had the courage to show himself in public again.

Mmadipetsane

In old tales found both in Africa and across the world, children are sometimes
warned very specifically against disobedience. This story from Lesotho, retold here by folklorist
MINNIE POSTMA *and illustrated by* LYN GILBERT, *is no exception.*

THE OLD PEOPLE tell the story of Mmadipetsane, the child who refused to listen to the warnings of adults:

One day Mmadipetsane's mother calls her. She calls, "Heee-laaa! Mmadipetsane!"

"Yes, Mme, I'm coming!" answers the girl.

When she arrives, her mother says to her, "Listen, dear child. Take the basket, the seroto, to collect some roots for us from the veld, and pick some wild spinach leaves for us to stew."

Mmadipetsane takes the basket and goes to the veld. It's a long way before she finds a spot where many wild roots grow. She digs and digs, and when she uncovers a root, she wipes it clean on a tuft of grass and puts it into the seroto.

Along comes the ledimo, the man-eating monster. He sees her. She sees him. He is very ugly. He is almost as big as a tree and darker than the blackest night. His teeth are the size of a boar's tusks.

"Heee-laaa, Mmadipetsane! What are you dig-digging?" he shouts, and his voice sounds like the noise the rainbird makes when he comes to lay his egg amongst the stones on the ground. But Mmadipetsane is not afraid of him. She doesn't even reply. Once again he calls, "Heee-laaa, Mmadipetsane, why are you dig-digging?"

This time she replies, in a voice that sounds like the wind blowing across the veld. "I am dig-digging the roots that belong to the ledimo and I am picking the young leaves of the spinach that grows near the dung-heap."

He strides towards her. He tries to catch and eat her, because he eats people. She darts away from him as quickly as a fieldmouse . . . and like a fieldmouse, she slips into a hole. The hole is too small for the ledimo, the big monster, and he can't catch her.

"Just you wait," he says in a loud voice. "I am clever, I shall find a way to catch you." And he smacks his lips

and he swallows so loudly that he sounds like the frogs when they jump into deep water: *duma-duma-duma!*

But Mmadipetsane laughs at him. She teases him. She taunts him and says that he looks like a creepy-crawly, a kgokgo. Teasing and taunting him, she sings:

"Sai kgokgo, sai kgokgokgo-kgo. Sai kgokgo, sai kgo-kgokgo-kgo . . . Sai! Sai!"

It hurts the ledimo's ears to hear her. It feels as though he has fleas biting the inside of his ears: "Sai! Sai! Sai!"

He walks back home, where he cannot hear her any longer.

Like a little fieldmouse, the naughty girl peeps out of the hole. When she sees that he has gone, she slips out quietly and scuttles between the grasses and the shrubs until she reaches her hae, her home.

"Here are the roots, Mme," she says.

"Where have you been, my child?"

"Ao, Mme we, I had to go very far, to the field of the ledimo."

"Jo – nna nna! Why do you not listen? Did the pigs bite off your ears when you were little? I told you to keep away from him."

"Tja!" answers the naughty child. "I am not afraid!"

"How can you not be afraid of him! He is bigger than any chief, he is stronger than any bull and he is more dangerous than the big water snake coiled up in the gleaming deep pool."

"Just look at me, Mmadipetsane. I am so small and weak, but I am cleverer than him," she retorts. "He cannot catch me, because I am as clever as the jackal, the phokojwe."

"What are you thinking, you disobedient child!" exclaims her mother.

"Mme, I know how the jackal works. I hide in the hole in the ground that the jackal has dug for me with his paws. But the ledimo, the Giant, the Strong One, the Dangerous One, cannot get inside. Then I tease him like this:

"Sai kgokgo, sai kgokgokgo-kgo. Sai kgokgo kgokgo-kgo-kgo . . . Sai! Sai! Sai!"

"What happens then, my child?"

"Then he is furious. He stomps the ground, like Pu-hu, the bull, with his hooves . . . and all I hear is *dump-dump-dump* as his feet pound the ground."

The woman warns her child once again, but Mmadipetsane does not take any notice of her. Early the next morning, while her mother is fetching water in the clay pot from the fountain, she takes her seroto and runs to the fields of the ledimo to dig for roots and to pick young leaves from the wild spinach that grows near the dungheap.

The ledimo sees her kneeling and digging.

"Heee-laaa, there! Why are you dig-digging so early in the morning, Mmadipetsane?"

"I am dig-digging the roots that belong to the ledimo and I am picking the wild spinach that grows in his fields!"

He charges towards her to catch her, but she glides as fast as a fieldmouse over grass and shrub to the hole which the jackal has dug for her. The ledimo cannot reach her. He is furious. He can smell her and this makes him long all the more for lovely, juicy human flesh. He can hear her voice coming from the hole: ". . . Sai kgokgo, sai kgokgokgo-kgo, sai, sai, sai!" It pierces him like arrows.

He is clever, though, the ledimo. He is even more cunning than the jackal, but Mmadipetsane does not know it. He is furious with her, but he does not say anything. He sits and waits outside the hole – like an old woman who sits and waits for her children to bring her food. He sits like a cat which waits for a mouse to come out of a hole.

But Mmadipetsane is even more cunning than he; she is as clever as the mouse. She is also sitting, waiting quietly. *Tu-u-u-u.*

Then the ledimo thinks of a plan to get her out.

"Mmadipetsane, you must come out now. The sun is shining high in the sky. Your mother is already standing on top of the big rock, the lefika, and she is looking for you. She is waiting for the roots and the wild spinach, because she is hungry!"

"Sai, sai, sai, sai – kgokgokgo-kgo!" she teases him. He is so furious that he falls to the ground, like a tree that the wind has blown over. He strikes the ground, *boom!* She knows that he is not dead and she sits as quietly as a mouse in the hole: *tu-u-u!* When she is hungry, she eats some of the roots that she has collected for her mother, but she does not move from her hiding place.

Now the ledimo has another idea. He tries to sound like her mother. In a high-pitched voice he says: "He-la, Mmadipetsane, my child! Where are you? The sun is setting over the tree tops in the west."

But Mmadipetsane is not stupid. She laughs at him and teases him: "Sai, sai, sai, kgokgokgo-kgo, sai, sai, sai, sai, kgokgokgo-kgo . . . Oh, are you my mother? You who are as ugly as a baboon, with teeth like a boar and with a stomach like a beer pot? Forget it!"

The ledimo sits quietly and listens to this. He thinks and thinks and thinks. That's it – he will make his voice even softer.

He calls her again: "Mmadipetsane! Darling, where are you? It's late, the sun is setting faster. It is now behind the branches of the trees . . ."

"Sai, sai, sai, kgo-kgo!" she teases. "Oh, are you my mother? Your voice is as rough as the rock face of the mountain! Mme's voice is smooth – as smooth as the fine sand that washes out at the water's edge! Sai, sai, sai, kgo-kgo," she laughs at him from inside the hole.

This time the ledimo calls softly, softly, softly. "Mmadipetsa-neee, come home. I am waiting for the roots and for the spinach leaves. The sun is touching the mountain tops in the west!"

But his voice is still strong and rough. It does not sound anything like the voice of a mother.

From deep inside the hole, Mmadipetsane answers, "Go to sleep, ledimo . . . I told you, when Mme speaks it sounds like tiny little grains of sand that would not hurt even a toddler's feet if he were to take his first steps on it."

And when the round, red sun falls behind the mountains in the west, she hears the ledimo walk home. As quietly as a mouse, she slips out of the hole and runs all the way home, to her hae.

That night the ledimo has a brilliant idea. In the dark he runs over the tufts of grass, like a hare, to the hole where Mmadipetsane always hides from him – from him, the Giant, the Strong One, the Dangerous One. With his huge hands, he fills the hole with stones . . . At the top, he leaves just enough room for Mmadipetsane's head. Then he goes to sleep.

Early the following morning, the disobedient child is once again dig-digging for roots in the ledimo's field. He leaves his house early to catch her. He shouts: "Heee-laaa, there! What are you dig-digging?"

"I am dig-digging the roots in the ledimo's field."

He is furious and charges at her. She runs away as fast as a fieldmouse to hide in the hole, but she does not know that it is almost filled with stones.

She tries to slip in safely, like a little mouse, but only her head fits in because of the stones. Her whole body sticks out.

"Ha-ha-ha-ha-ha!" laughs the ledimo in his rough voice that sounds like rocks rolling off the mountain. "Ha-ha-ha-ha!" laughs the ledimo and smacks his lips, with a sound like children diving and splashing in the pool. Then the ledimo, the Giant, the Strong One, the Dangerous One, grabs the child who would not listen to her mother's warning.

He puts her in a bag and Mmadipetsane cries: "Hiii-ii-hiiiii, I'll never do it again, until I am old . . . until the day my legs fold under me from old age . . . until my teeth have all fallen out like the leaves . . . until my eyes are blue like those of the white people, I shall never come to dig for roots here. Hiiii . . . please let me go!"

But the ledimo does not listen. He does not even hear her cry. He only hears her teasing . . .

"Sai, sai, sai, kgokgokgo-kgo!"

He knots the bag and throws it over his shoulder and walks to his hae, his home, where he will eat her.

This is the end of the story of a disobedient child and her punishment.

Translator: LEILA LATIMER

Kamiyo of the River

In this story from the Transkei, recorded and retold by HUGH TRACEY, *a theme is depicted that also appears in various guises in the folklore of other indigenous language groups: a statue or other inanimate object changes into a living being, or vice versa. The illustration is by* DIEK GROBLER.

ONCE UPON A TIME there was a man who had plenty of cattle and sheep and goats, but one thing was lacking: he could not find himself a wife.

One day he was walking down the valley by the river when he said to himself, "I really must find myself a wife, or I shall be getting too old. What can I do?"

Then he sat down beside the river, and on the other bank he saw a large tree with beautiful green leaves on it.

"Ah!" he said. "Supposing I take that tree and carve myself a statue of a beautiful young woman."

And that is exactly what he did. He took his axe, and his adze, and carved from the tree the image of a lovely woman. When he had finished, she looked so beautiful that he breathed into her nostrils, touched her eyes – and at once she came alive.

"Ah!" he said. "Here's my wife at last!"

Then he said to her, "You must never tell anyone where you come from. If anyone should ask you, you must just say, 'I am Kamiyo – Kamiyo of the river.'"

And so he took her home. He gave her the married woman's head-ring to wear, an apron, beautiful clothes and beads – everything she wanted. So they lived very happily together at his home.

Now, one day, some young men came past and saw Kamiyo, and said, "How can such an old man have such a beautiful young wife? It's not right. We will take her away to our own village."

So they caught hold of her and took her away to their village on the other side of the hill.

The husband was very sad that the strong young men had taken away his wife and wondered what he could do.

Then he had an idea. He had two pigeons, and he called them to him and said, "Pigeons, you will fly for me across the hill, to the village where they have taken my wife, and you shall sing her a song I will teach you, and then you will bring back to me her apron."

So the two pigeons learnt the song, flew across the hill, landed on the fence around the yard where the girl was held prisoner by the young men, and they sang:

Kamiyo, Kamiyo,
We are sent by your husband.
Kamiyo, Kamiyo,
He said we must come here,
Kamiyo, Kamiyo,
And bring him your apron, your apron.

Now when the young men heard the pigeons singing, they said, "All right! Give them your apron. We have plenty more. All we want is you."

So she gave the pigeons her apron, and they flew back with it to her husband.

The next day the husband said to the pigeons, "Today you must go and ask for her head-ring."

So they flew over the hill, landed on the fence again, and sang:

Kamiyo, Kamiyo,
We are sent by your husband.
Kamiyo, Kamiyo,
He said we must come here,
Kamiyo, Kamiyo,
And bring him your head-ring, your head-ring.

And the young men said, "Give them the head-ring. We don't want it; we only want you."

So she gave the pigeons her head-ring, and they flew back again.

Each day the pigeons flew across the hill and asked her for something else, for everything she had, until finally the husband said, "Now, my pigeons, you must go and ask for her life."

So the pigeons flew back once more. This time they landed on her lap as she sat outside the hut, and they sang:

Kamiyo, Kamiyo,
We are sent by your husband.
Kamiyo, Kamiyo,
He said we must come here,
Kamiyo, Kamiyo,
And bring him your life, your life.

And as they sang, they both pecked at her eyes, and immediately Kamiyo turned back into a statue.

First her feet fell away, and then her legs; then her arms fell away, and then her head; and last of all, her body rolled slowly down, down the slope, all the way down to the river.

And the moment it touched the water, she turned back into a tree, and put out green leaves again, and that is where Kamiyo has been ever since, to this day.

Spider and the Crows

The spider plays a dramatic role in many African stories. He is often exceptionally resourceful – as is evident in this Nigerian folk tale. In the stories of the Ashanti he is known as Kwaku Anansi. The illustrator is VÉRONIQUE TADJO.

LONG AGO THERE WAS A GREAT FAMINE in a certain land and no one had anything to eat; no one, that is, except the crows. Every day they flew a great distance to pick figs from a tree that stood in the middle of a wide river. Then they brought the fruit home to eat.

When Spider heard about this, he immediately thought of an ingenious plan. He smeared his hindquarters with beeswax, took a potsherd and went to the crows on the pretext of borrowing a burning coal.

The crows were busy eating when he arrived and all around them on the ground lay figs.

"Morning, dear friends," said Spider, sitting down carefully on one of the delicious figs. "Could you give me a burning coal?"

Taking the burning coal, Spider thanked the crows and walked away with the fig firmly attached to his sticky hindquarters.

The crows did not suspect anything because the cunning thief, pretending to be courteous, walked backwards as he left them.

At home, Spider extinguished the burning coal and quickly went back to the crows to ask for more fire. This time Spider chose the largest and ripest fig and, after some time, walked away cheekily with his spoils.

And then he did it a third time. But now the birds were beginning to get suspicious. "Why do you keep coming to get a burning coal from us?" they asked.

"By the time I get home, the coal is burnt out. This happens every time," answered Spider.

"You are lying!" said the oldest crow. "I'm sure you put it out so that you have an excuse to return here again. You are just after our food, you sly creature!"

Spider began to cry bitterly. "Oh, no! That's not true! The coal burnt itself out. Oh! Ever since my parents died, life has been difficult for me. When they were still alive, my parents assured me that if ever I needed any-

thing I should ask their friends, the crows. Yes, that's just what they said. And now, look how you treat me," he sobbed.

"Oh, stop crying now!" said the oldest crow, picking up a fig. "Take this and go home. If you come back again tomorrow morning at daybreak, we'll take you to the fig tree."

"Thank you kindly, dear friends," said Spider and ran home as fast as his legs could carry him.

That night, just as the crows were dozing off, Spider took a bundle of straw and made a large fire near the birds' nest.

"It's morning! It's morning!" called Spider as the flames rose high in the sky. "Just look how red the sun has made the eastern sky."

But the oldest crow answered, "No, Spider, you made a fire. Wait until you hear the cock crow."

Spider crept into the hen-house and disturbed the fowls until the hens began to cackle and the large cock crowed.

"Wake up! It's morning!" he called out.

"Trickster! *You* have woken the fowls, Spider!" answered the oldest crow. "Come, let us rather wait until we hear the first call to prayer."

"Allah is great! Allah is great!" called Spider from behind a bush.

But the oldest crow said, "No, I recognise that voice. It's you who called, Spider. Go home and stay there! I'll call you when the sun rises."

All Spider could do was wait. He went home and fell asleep.

Eventually, when it began to get light, the crows woke him and each crow gave him a feather.

With his borrowed feathers, Spider flew with the crows to the fig tree in the middle of the wide river. But every time one of the crows wanted to pick a fig he shrieked, "No, you can't! I saw it first! It's mine!"

And then he would take the fig and put it in his bag. Things continued in this way until there was no fruit left on the tree. Spider picked all the figs for himself and the crows got none.

"Now I know that you really are a trickster!" said the oldest crow. Angrily, the crows snatched back the feathers that they had lent him and flew away, leaving him alone.

And there Spider stayed, all alone in the fig tree, completely surrounded by water. And for the first time in his life, he didn't know what to do.

Later when darkness descended, he began to cry.

"If I don't want to stay here in the tree for the rest of my life, I'll just have to jump into the air like the crows," Spider said to himself at last.

He took a deep breath and . . . *plop!* He fell into the water right amongst the crocodiles!

"And what do we have here?" asked an old crocodile. "Can we eat it?"

"Don't be ridiculous!" Spider answered quickly and he began to sob. "I'm one of you. Don't you know that everyone has been searching for me for years? I ran away in the days of your grandfathers, when I was very small. And no one has ever found me. You are the first of my family members I've met."

Spider cried so hard that the tears splashed on the ground. The crocodiles themselves cried crocodile tears. "You poor thing!" they cried, sniffing loudly. "Don't worry, you can stay here with us, in the hole on the bank where we lay our eggs."

But one of the crocodiles was suspicious and examined Spider very carefully. "We must first make sure that he really is one of us," he thought.

"Come, let's give the stranger a little mud soup," he said quietly to another crocodile. "If he drinks it, then we'll know he speaks the truth. If he doesn't want it, we'll know that he tells lies and he is definitely not one of us."

And so it was done.

When Spider saw the gourd of mud soup, he pretended that he was very excited. "Where did you find this delicious recipe of my grandmother's?" he asked, pretending to drink the soup. But he quietly dug a hole with his back feet and made a tiny hole in the bottom of the gourd with his front feet.

"That was delicious!" he declared, putting the gourd behind him while the concoction oozed into the ground.

"Well, he's definitely one of us," the crocodiles said to each other when they saw the empty gourd. So they allowed Spider to sleep in the hole together with a group of small crocodiles and a hundred and one crocodile eggs.

Before Spider crept in, he said, "Remember now, children, if you hear a *plop* in the night, don't be afraid. It will just be me burping as a result of your mother's delicious mud soup."

When all the crocodiles were asleep, Spider took an egg and threw it into the fire.

Plop! The egg burst open.

"That's the strange grandfather-uncle of ours burping," said the little crocodiles to each other.

And the large crocodiles who overheard them said, "Quiet, children, one mustn't speak about family like that!"

But Spider said, "Leave them alone. They are my grandchildren. They can say what they like."

So he baked the eggs in the fire, one after the other, and ate every single one. All through the night the crocodiles heard *plop* every now and then. And every time someone said, "It's just our strange grandfather-uncle who is burping."

By morning, there was only one egg left.

When the adult crocodiles asked the young ones to turn the eggs, Spider said quickly, "Don't worry, I've done it already."

Then the crocodiles suggested that the eggs be counted.

"I'll bring them out one at a time for you," said Spider.

He brought the egg out of the hole, put it in front of the crocodiles, and the crocodiles made a mark on it.

Spider disappeared into the hole again, licked off the mark and brought it back. Again the crocodiles marked the egg.

And so he carried the same egg back and forth.

"Two . . . three . . . four . . ." the crocodiles counted the eggs until they reached one hundred and one.

"All of our eggs are still there," they said every day, entirely satisfied.

"I'm so glad I have found my blood relatives again," said Spider one day. "But I want to go and fetch my wife and children, so that we can all be together."

"Go and do so," said the crocodiles. "But come back quickly so that you can play with us again and help us count the eggs."

"Of course," said Spider, the trickster. "It's a great game, isn't it? If you help me to cross the river, I'll come back very soon."

The crocodiles put him in a canoe, and two of them rowed him away.

But one of the pair, who thought further than his long snout, did not trust the situation. When they were in the middle of the river, he turned around and said, "Wait a minute. I'm coming back now. I just want to go and check the eggs."

And thus the crocodiles discovered the one marked egg.

"Such a trickster!" they screamed. "Bring him back immediately! He is not one of us!" they shouted across the river.

But the crocodile who was rowing the canoe was a bit deaf.

"Listen!" Spider said to the rower. "They say you must hurry. It's nearly high tide," and he spurred the crocodile on until he was safely on the other side. And so he got clean away.

Translator: DIANNE STEWART

Natiki

This Namaqualand story, with its echoes of the European Cinderella tale, is retold by
GLAUDIEN KOTZÉ, who heard it as a child from a much-loved Nama storyteller called Tryntjie Koekas.
Kotzé describes her as a "masterly storyteller". The illustration is by NIKOLAAS DE KAT.

THE KALAHARI EVENING SUN sinks away behind the thorn trees. The hunters come back from the veld. At the kraal people are talking and laughing.

Natiki's two sisters and her mother rub their bodies with fat. They are making themselves beautiful, because tonight is the dance of the full moon.

Natiki's heart is burning to go along to the big dance as well, but when she asks her mother whether she can go too, her mother only says, "Go and fetch the goats, and make sure you bring them in before nightfall. Bring along some wood and make a big fire so that the wild animals will stay away."

Her mother and her two sisters treat Natiki very, very badly. They are jealous of her because she is more beautiful than her two older sisters. And they are afraid that a young hunter might take a fancy to *her* at the dance.

So Natiki goes out into the veld. By the time she comes back to the kraal with the goats, her mother and sisters have already left for the dance.

She places the handful of porcupine quills she has collected on the wall of the cooking enclosure. She breaks up the wood. She lays the fire and lights it.

Next, she rubs fat on her body until her skin looks like burnished copper. She brushes her hair with a thorn twig and rubs a yellow mixture of crushed bark and fat on her face. Around her neck are beads made of ostrich eggshell. She threads strings of beads through her hair and ties dried springbok ears filled with seeds onto her legs. Last of all she places the porcupine quills in her little leather pouch.

The moon is already high when she sets off along the path. Here and there, as she walks, she sticks a porcupine quill into the ground.

When she comes to the top of the rise and sees the big fire of the dance, she starts to feel a bit nervous.

What will her mother and sisters say? But then she smells the meat on the coals and her feet skip this way and that, and the springbok ears go *shirr-shirr* around her ankles.

When she gets to the fire, she stands to one side at first. Then she catches sight of her mother and her sisters. But they are wondering, along with the other women, who has arrived at the party so alone, and a stranger.

Natiki goes to stand with the women who are singing and clapping their hands. She joins in the singing. She claps her hands and her feet are light. A young hunter smiles at her as he dances past. His eyes rest on her.

When it starts getting late, Natiki's sisters begin to yawn – gaping yawns that make them look even uglier. Natiki's mother sizes things up and then she says to her two eldest daughters, "Just take some more meat for yourselves, and then we'll walk home." And then they are gone.

Natiki sings and claps her hands with the other women for a long, long while. When they are all exhausted, the young hunter approaches her. "I'll walk with you," he says.

As they follow the porcupine quills on the way to her mother's hut, Natiki tells him everything about her two sisters and her mother who treat her so badly. And how angry her mother would be if she realised that Natiki had gone along to the dance.

Then the hunter says, "I will take you away from them. I will discuss this matter with your mother myself."

The mother and the sisters hear the voices approaching from afar.

"It must be her coming home with one of the hunters," says the younger sister.

"No, who would want to walk with *her*?" asks the eldest sister, who is very jealous of Natiki.

Natiki and the young hunter appear in the red blaze of the fire. She looks really beautiful.

"You awful child, what do you think you're doing?" her mother scolds her.

When the young hunter sees that Natiki is starting to tremble, he turns to face her mother. "I am taking Natiki away tonight, for good," he says. "And I will make sure that her pots are never empty."

"You will see how useless she is!" shouts her mother and jumps up to separate Natiki and the hunter. But Natiki is too quick for her. She jumps out of the way and goes to stand behind the hunter. Now there is nothing that her mother can do.

So Natiki leaves with the hunter to the place of his own people, far far away.

Every afternoon when her mother and sisters come trudging back with big loads of wood on their backs, the two sisters grumble, "Natiki, Natiki, one day we will get you back."

But Natiki is joyful and happy. She looks after her husband and children well.

And it is just as the hunter promised: there is always meat in her pots.

Translator: MARGARET AUERBACH

The Hare and the Tree Spirit

*The hare, usually a cunning, impish character, features in countless African tales, with such
diverse names as Kalulu, Sunguru and Mvundlazana. In this Xhosa story, retold by PHYLLIS SAVORY,
the hare – unusually for him – does someone a favour. The illustrator is LYN GILBERT.*

ONE MORNING, IN THE EARLY HOURS, a scraggy old woman was returning home from a nearby village, where she had attended a marriage feast. Not noticing a broken pot that lay on the path, she stumbled over it and fell, cutting her leg on a broken edge.

"Curses on the fool who left his rubbish in the path where decent folk walk!" she exclaimed as she picked herself up. "May his first-born be struck dumb this very minute, and remain so until someone breaks the spell by doing a thing as foolish as he who left this broken pot in the path to afflict me!"

And she continued on her way.

Not far away lived a hard working man named Dondo, his wife and their seven-year-old daughter, Tembe. The ageing couple had toiled for many years to secure the comfort they now enjoyed, and life had been good to them in all but one thing: it had given them only one child, a daughter. Imagine their distress when they discovered that morning that she had been struck dumb overnight.

"Who could have cast this wicked spell on her?" they asked each other.

The many medicine men they consulted were unable to help the child, and so the years went by. She grew in grace and beauty, but it became apparent that there was little hope of any riches in the form of the lobola, the marriage cattle, that should have been their due for a daughter of such diligence, grace and beauty. This distressed the ageing parents greatly, because who, they argued, would pay for a dumb wife?

How true their fears proved to be, for news of the girl's affliction had spread far and wide, and none came to seek her hand. There was one, however, a youth named Nthu, whose heart was touched by her beauty to such an extent that he longed to help her.

"Surely," he thought to himself, "if I offer a suitable

gift to the tree spirits, they will take pity on this lovely girl and cast off the spell that has tied her tongue."

Nthu waited until nightfall so that none would know of his errand. Then he visited a large euphorbia tree that grew nearby and poured out the tale of the girl's trouble to the spirits of the tree.

Now, Mvundla the Hare had his home well hidden at the foot of this particular tree and when his slumbers were disturbed by Nthu's pleadings, he listened with interest. He decided to have some fun at Nthu's expense, hoping to benefit himself at the same time.

So he tried to make his voice sound gruff as he replied, "You who ask this of me, what payment have you to offer?"

"Good Spirit," answered Nthu after a pause, "ask what you will and I shall gladly pay, for my heart aches for this lovely maiden."

"We-ell," said the hare, pretending to give the matter due consideration, "I would have you bring me a good supply of fresh green vegetables and tasty berries every day, to be left here at my feet, and I shall consider the matter."

And sure enough, day after day the hopeful Nthu brought a fine supply of fresh green food and laid it at the foot of the big euphorbia tree, and day after day the hare enjoyed his delicious free meals. However, there came a time when his conscience began to prick him,

for he was not a bad hare. He decided to make the acquaintance of the afflicted girl and try to cure her dumbness, for he had a particularly good opinion of his own abilities.

On the following morning, he went to Dondo's millet lands, which he knew well because he had often robbed them in the past. There he found the girl, Tembe, carefully planting rows of young millet seedlings. She took no notice of him when he asked if he could help her, but continued with her work.

Then an idea struck him. He picked up some of the seedlings that were lying in a heap and followed her, planting a row of his own behind her. But he planted them upside down, with their roots waving in the air. At least she would take notice of him now, he thought.

When Tembe reached the end of her row, she straightened her back and turned to begin the next row. Then she caught sight of what the hare had done. She shook her fist at him and shouted, "Oh, you fool, what do you think you're doing?"

A look of astonishment spread over her face as she realised that her voice had returned to her! Throwing down her hoe, she ran shouting and laughing to find her parents.

"So like humans," grumbled the hare. "Never a word of thanks. But how long, I wonder, would Nthu have continued to supply me with such delicious free meals?"

The Mantis and the Moon

The praying mantis, also called Kaggen, is one of the most important
figures in San folklore. This mantis story by children's book author and novelist
Marguerite Poland is illustrated by Marna Hattingh.

THERE WAS ONCE A MANTIS who tried to catch the moon. He wished to sit on it and cross the sky each night so that all the animals would say, "There is the mantis travelling on the moon. He must surely be a god and we should praise him."

Then the mantis could ride majestically at last, looking down on the great dry desert where he lived: at the camelthorns and empty water courses and the herds of springbok gazing up at him. He would be proud, for they would think he really was a god, and every creature would revere him. But the mantis was just an insect and the moon was far away. Even the night birds whose shadows dipped across the moon's face would never reach it, so how could a mantis fly there – he with the short, whirring wings? Still, the mantis was a dreamer, and when he sat rocking back and forth on a twig, or cupped in a leaf, he thought only of the moon and a way to get there.

The moon was elusive, for it did not always rise at the same time. The mantis decided to catch it as it peered over the horizon – then it was big and cumbersome, and clambered slowly into the sky. For when it was high and white it was distant, moving swiftly, and often it disappeared before it reached the far horizon, becoming faint and white like a fragment of forgotten cloud in the rising light of the sun.

The mantis waited impatiently all day until the shadows crept out from under the stones and bushes. He watched until the sky was pale green where the last daylight and the blue darkness met. And when the moon rose, it came so silently he nearly missed it. There it was, caught in the branches of a camelthorn.

The mantis flew to the tree in short, urgent bursts. He hurried up the trunk, half running, half flying, climbing between the thorns and the drooping fronds of tiny oval leaves. The moon was above him, pinned by

the topmost twigs. He struggled upwards and pounced, but he overbalanced and when he steadied himself to spring again, the moon had gone. It was cradled in the branches of a baobab – resting quietly, it seemed, waiting for the mantis to unharness it.

The mantis flew with a whirr and a click of wings to the foot of the baobab which stretched up its mighty branches to tangle with the stars. He started up the trunk – a long journey for a small creature. But when he reached the cradle of the tree, the moon had climbed ahead and was anchored to the branches high above him. The mantis flew towards the moon, determined to catch it before it broke loose. But when he got there it was gone, moving on, smaller and swifter and very far away.

As the moon waned, it rose later each night. The mantis was drowsy with watching, and too slow to reach it. There were times when there was no moon at all and the desert creatures were uneasy. For although the moon always returned to light their grazing grounds, slim and curved and supple as a hunting-bow, perhaps, one night, it would just keep on falling into the great wastes of sky below the earth and never turn and rise again over the desert.

The mantis tried to catch the young new moon, but it was lithe and swift and even the acacias could not hold it with their sharp white thorns.

"I shall make a trap," declared the mantis, and he wove a rope out of dry grass and tied it in a noose around a stick. He hid among some rocks on a high ridge so that he would be above the moon when it rose – full and orange and as heavy as a calabash of thick, sour milk. When his noose was silhouetted against the moon, the mantis tugged – for surely the rope would tighten round it long enough for him to scramble up. But the noose knotted on itself and fell empty to the ground. The moon rose higher, undisturbed.

The mantis crept into a bush to think and there he pondered, brown as the dead leaves caught in its tangled stems. Somehow he must catch the moon and ride on it. How else could one so small be a god? There was no other way to be noticed and praised by the animals.

He cut a stake and sharpened it and set it on the hilltop. It would pierce the moon and hold it, like a big white baobab flower caught on a thorn.

Again the mantis hid as the moon rose above the ridge of hills. It moved slowly towards the stake.

"Oh, foolish moon!" he cried. "Now I have caught you! Oh, wise and cunning Mantis!" But the stake only traced a shadow on the moon's face and then the moon was gone, climbing higher, up into the night.

The mantis shouted with rage and broke the stake in two. He went to plan another way to outwit the moon.

He made a djani, a length of reed and a partridge feather tied to a short twist of sinew, weighted with a stone. Tossed into the air, it would spiral to the ground, fast as a falling star. Surely it would twist itself around the moon and bring it down?

When the moon was new, a small sickle he could easily capture, he took his djani up into the tallest baobab and waited. When the rising moon was level with his hiding place, he flung the djani at it. It flew like a whip, curling across the curve of the moon. Then it dropped gently, the feather fluttering like a small, falling bird. The mantis yanked the stone from the djani and threw it on the ground.

The moon became full once more and the mantis followed it to see where it went when it sank below the horizon. He flew from bush to bush, from stone to stone, watching it travel across the sky. He came upon a waterhole deep in the sand, trampled by many hooves – and there, far below, was the moon, caught in the water.

Stealthily he crept down the steep bank to where the

coarse, dark sand was damp. He paused, gazing at the bright, hovering disc. He pounced on it, clutching at it with his spiny claws. But he sank gasping under the water, then struggled to the bank wet and afraid. And still the moon lay there, bright and glowing.

Many times the mantis tried to pry the moon out of the water, but he failed. At last, in anger, he took a rock and hurled it, cursing the moon.

The stone shattered the reflection and a thousand splinters of moonlight pierced the mantis's eyes. Blind with pain, he ran away and hid in a thorn tree. He could not ease the splinters from his eyes and in everything he saw were brilliant beams of moonlight. He could not sleep: there was no darkness in which to rest. He no longer wished to be a god and sit astride the moon so that the desert animals would praise him – he wondered how he ever could have hoped for that.

He crept up the thorn tree to where the branches reached into the warm evening air. He waited there until the moon rose – to him, a great fragmented light. He held out his front legs to it, folded up because he was praying, and he begged the moon to give him back his sight.

He swayed gently on a twig, his head bent, a small and humble insect.

And the moon kept on rising, higher and whiter than before. Then at last it set at the edge of the desert's barren wastes, and still the mantis sat, bowing to it as he prayed.

When daylight came, the moon appeared pale and steady and the shadows of the thorn trees fell sharply on the sand; bird-flight was clear and swift and the mantis knew the moon had taken all the splinters from his eyes.

That was long ago, when the great herds wandered freely from the sea to the vast, dry plains of the Heikum people. But the children of the mantis live there still, brown and green as the leaves that change with the seasons. And they sit, their forelegs held up in praise of the moon who forgave and restored the sight of their ancestor – the small, short-winged one, who wished to be a god.

The Snake with Seven Heads

The breaking of a curse in order for someone to be set free or to take on his own form again is a popular theme in African folk tales. In this Xhosa story an important role is played by the number seven – which, like the number three, is considered to have magical qualities. The story is retold here by GCINA MHLOPHE, children's book author and a masterly storyteller onstage. The illustrator is NATALIE HINRICHSEN.

Sukela ngantsomi
Chosi

THERE ONCE WAS A WOMAN called Manjuza, who had two special talents. Her singing voice was rich and strong and people loved to hear her sing. To see Manjuza dance, though, was the very best thing to brighten one's day. People came from near and far to invite Manjuza to dance for them on important days of celebration, and she was best known as a wedding dancer. A wedding without Manjuza to stand up at the right time – when the bride was about to come out, looking her best, smelling of beautiful herbs and her face glowing like the morning sun – that wedding was no wedding at all. Indeed, a wedding without Manjuza was a wedding soon forgotten.

Guleni, where Manjuza lived, was a small village of humble, hard-working people. Although it was small, it was well known for its brave hunters. The leader of the hunting band, Mthiyane, was a respected man who spoke only when he had something really important to say. He had been a good hunter since his youth, and many mothers had hoped he would marry their daughters. But when he married Manjuza, everyone had to agree that they made an excellent couple.

As the years passed, the couple had three children, two boys and a girl. When Mthiyane was away with his hunting band, sometimes for weeks on end, he would sit quietly under the starlit sky and wonder what Manjuza was doing at home with the children. How he missed hearing the soft breathing of the children drifting off to sleep after the evening meal, with their mother's voice softly singing lullabies to them.

One morning, Manjuza was alone in the house. She was busy preparing beer, for her husband was coming home in two days and she wanted the beer to be ready for him. While she was working, she heard somebody calling from outside. An old woman had come to ask her to dance at her granddaughter's wedding. But Manjuza had a problem: she had already agreed to dance at another wedding on that day.

The old woman tried all she could think of to persuade Manjuza to cancel the other wedding appointment, but Manjuza had given her word and would not change her mind. She asked the old woman to change the day of the wedding so she could dance at both weddings and nobody would be disappointed. But the old woman refused to change the day of her granddaughter's wedding and she was very angry with Manjuza. Before she left, she spitefully threatened Manjuza that she would cast a curse on her husband. Something terrible would happen to Mthiyane on his way home and he would turn into an ugly monster.

After the old woman had left, Manjuza sat alone, feeling very tired. Her heart was filled with pain. She was a kind person who had always enjoyed her dancing because she loved to see the happy faces of the wedding guests.

On the night Manjuza was expecting her husband's return, the children were very excited. They sat up and waited for him long after they had finished their supper. It was getting late. They waited for a knock on the door, but it did not come. They waited to hear the barking of the dogs that ran ahead of the hunting band, but all was quiet. The children began to yawn and, one by one, fell asleep. Their mother sat, unable to sleep.

It was just before dawn when Mthiyane came home. How strange he looked! His eyes had turned a shiny grey and they were flashing this way and that – like those of an angry snake. His tongue was hanging out of his mouth and had grown very long. He did not say a word, but he was making very strange noises.

Manjuza was too terrified to say anything. Her mouth went dry as she watched her beloved husband turn into a snake with seven heads. She had to think fast. Already the cocks were crowing and the sky was turning bright orange in the east. She had to hide the snake somewhere before the children woke up.

Quickly she cleared one of the huts that was used to store food at harvest time. In the hut there was a big black pot which was used for storing grain. She emptied it and let the snake crawl into the pot. She broke a piece from the lid on one side to make a hole for him to breathe. Then she carefully gave food to each of the seven heads before she locked the hut.

When the children woke, they asked for their father. Manjuza told them he had not yet arrived but would be home in a few days.

When evening came, she put the children to sleep and quietly went out to feed the snake. Only after she had locked the storeroom and gone to bed did she break down and cry herself to sleep.

That night, Manjuza had a dream. Her grandmother appeared in her dream, telling her that all she had to do to break the curse was to dance at seven weddings. When she came back from the seventh wedding she would find her husband in the body he had had before the curse had been spoken. But it was very important to keep all this a secret, even from her own children.

Manjuza's children could not understand why their father had not come home from his hunting trip. Nor could they understand why their mother got angry with them whenever they asked why she had started to keep one of the huts locked, or why she seemed so troubled.

Still Manjuza kept her secret and continued to feed the snake. She was very unhappy to see how much the children were missing their father. At times they wondered whether he had died and their mother was afraid

to tell them. But, on occasion, they would see her putting some food aside. When they asked her why, she said it was for their father, in case he came home.

As usual, people came to invite Manjuza to dance at their weddings and she gladly accepted. The first wedding passed, and the second, and the third . . . Of course, she was counting each one. She could not think about anything but weddings. Each time she went away to dance she fed the snake, locked the hut and took the key with her. Often the children begged her to show them what was in that hut. She refused. They even planned to steal the key, but Manjuza was very careful.

More invitations came and Manjuza went to dance. Each invitation brought her closer to the seventh wedding. When she came back from the sixth one, she was so happy she could not stop smiling. Her face was bright and her eyes shone like those of a young girl in love. She looked at the puzzled faces of her children and thought to herself, "Soon they'll be smiling too."

When the invitation came for the seventh wedding, she could not contain her joy. She sang to herself and laughed aloud, until her neighbours thought she must have fallen in love with another man. When they asked her who it was, she just laughed.

On the day of the seventh wedding, Manjuza woke up early, made breakfast for the children and then took her time getting dressed. She wanted to look her best. In the meantime, the children were again planning to steal the key. They tried so many tricks to take the key that Manjuza was angry by the time she left, but it was not like her to be careless about such an important thing: she took the key with her.

The children, disappointed, grumbled while they ate their breakfast. Then they went out to play. In the early afternoon they were playing and chasing each other when they found themselves in front of the hut they were forbidden to enter. The eldest boy tried the door they had tried so often before. It was open. Manjuza had taken the key but forgotten to lock the door!

Carefully they looked around the inside of the hut. It was empty except for a big black three-legged pot with a broken lid. They looked at each other, unable to understand why their mother had hidden a pot. The eldest boy lifted the heavy lid to see what was inside. The huge snake with seven heads stared back at him. Screaming in terror, the children ran out.

Manjuza's house was not far from the river, and the strange snake slid out of the pot and slithered down to the river bank. There it lay in the afternoon sun and gazed at its own reflection in the water.

Manjuza's children ran to tell their friends about the strange snake. A band of young boys and girls set off to find it. When they reached the spot where the snake lay, they stood open-mouthed. The seven heads looked at them with great interest, too. One of the heads said, "Wo gigigi, here they stand."

"What do they want?" asked the second head.

"They are staring at us," remarked the third.

"I think they want to see our heads," the fourth said.

"Why don't they come closer?" asked the fifth.

"I think they are s cared of being bitten," the sixth said.

"Can't they be bitten where they stand?" the seventh asked.

The children turned and ran as fast as their feet would carry them. They rushed home and told their parents about the snake with seven heads. The men took their sticks and went to the river. When they got there, they all stood as if under a spell. They had found it hard to imagine a snake with more than one head, but when it started talking they were dumbstruck.

Of course, they did not want to say that they were

scared — it would be a disgrace to admit that to their wives and children. Some men said it was not right to kill the snake. They said, "Perhaps our ancestors are trying to tell us something. Maybe it is better to go home and discuss the matter in a village meeting."

The women knew right away that the men were making excuses to hide their fear. They wanted the snake dead before sunset, because they were worried for the safety of their children.

The men said, "We too care about the children, but the snake at the river is no ordinary snake!"

The women would not listen to reason. They gathered to cook pots full of soft porridge. A long line of mothers carrying hot porridge on their heads went down to the river. By this time the snake was angry and talking very fast.

"Wo gigigi, here come the women now!"

"What do they want?"

"They are coming towards us . . ."

"Those pots . . ."

Before the angry heads could continue, the women rushed forward and poured the hot porridge on the snake. Large blisters burst open on its skin and it moaned in agony. More people arrived from the village to help kill the snake. They started to sing a song, rejoicing that they had killed the snake with many heads:

> *Siyibulel' inyok' enamakhanda-khanda,*
> *Thina siyibulele,*
> *Wo gi, agigigi,*
> *Inyok' enamakhanda-khanda . . .*

Manjuza was on her way back from the seventh wedding when she heard the women singing the new song. She was terrified. The villagers had killed her husband! She felt tears spring to her eyes.

What should she do? Even though she dreaded the thought, she decided to go and join the jubilant singing and dancing until she could work out what to do next. It was getting dark and the people would not see her tearful face.

But as she drew closer and looked over the people's shoulders she saw, slowly rising from the blistered green skin of the dead snake, her dear husband. His face was rumpled and his eyes half-closed, as if he had been sleeping for a long, long time.

The singing stopped. Everyone was shocked at the inexplicable return of Manjuza's husband.

Mthiyane looked at the villagers in a daze and started moving towards the crowd to look for his wife.

Manjuza could not believe her eyes. She ran forward and threw her arms around her husband's neck. She was crying and laughing with relief.

Mthiyane held his wife close. He could not understand what was going on around him. Then their children ran forward, and the family was together again. The sun had set and the end of the day had signalled the end of the curse.

Manjuza began to sing and dance, more beautifully than she had ever sung and danced before, and the whole village rejoiced with her.

Phela phela ngantsomi.

The Hare's Revenge

The hare – like the tortoise – appears in countless African folk tales as an excellent illustration of the principle that those who are not strong must be clever instead. In this Zambian tale, retold by PHYLLIS SAVORY and illustrated by MARNA HATTINGH, the hare yet again manages to outwit a far bigger animal. Furthermore, in this story he plays a role that is traditionally filled by the honey-badger.

ONE DAY, IN EARLY SPRING, the buffalo was on his way to pay his yearly visit to his chief, the lion, as the law of the land required him to do. On the way he met the hare sauntering along the road.

"Hare," said the buffalo, "I want you to come with me to visit King Lion."

"No, Buffalo," replied the hare, "I do not trust Lion. He is a big, fierce fellow, and I am afraid he might eat me. No, I cannot go with you."

"But Hare," replied the buffalo, "King Lion is a very great friend of mine, and he will listen to me. I promise he will not harm you."

"Why do you want me to go with you, Buffalo?"

"Hare, I want you to carry my sleeping mat. It is not proper that such an important animal as I should carry his own mat. I shall reward you well."

"Very well, Buffalo, I shall go with you. Give me your sleeping mat, and I shall carry it."

The buffalo put his mat on the hare's shoulders, and they proceeded to the lion's village. The sun was very hot and the hare soon became tired, for the sleeping mat was heavy. "Please, good friend, help me with this load," he said. "I am only a little one, and your mat is very heavy."

"Stop grumbling, Hare. You are a lazy fellow!" bellowed the buffalo in such a loud voice that the hare was too frightened to say anything more. He trudged along in silence behind the buffalo.

At midday the buffalo lay down to rest in the shade of a tree and the hare thankfully put down his load, for the sun was fierce. While they were resting, a honey-bird flew across their path and began calling for them to rob a bees' nest nearby.

Now, the hare was particularly fond of honey. So in spite of his aching legs, he followed the bird to the bees' nest, which was in a hole in the ground. He opened up

the hole and ate as much honey as he could cram into his mouth. Then he returned to continue his rest under the shady tree. But just then the buffalo woke up and at once lifted the heavy sleeping mat onto the hare's shoulders, saying that they had to hurry or they would not reach the lion's village before dark.

As they were leaving, a thought struck the hare and he turned to retrace his steps to the bees' nest.

"Where are you going?" called the buffalo.

"Oh," replied the hare, "I have decided to fill this little calabash with honey, that we may eat it to restore our strength along the way. You go on, my friend, I'll catch up with you later."

So the buffalo continued along the path.

But the hare had been smarting more and more under the buffalo's treatment and had devised a plan to punish him. He filled his little calabash with honey and then he unrolled the sleeping mat. Collecting a great many bees, he spread them over the mat, which he rolled up again. Then he hurried after the buffalo and they continued on their journey.

The hare's shoulders were very sore and bruised by the time they reached the lion's village, but he said nothing. The lion received them kindly. After a good meal he showed them to a hut in which they were to spend the night. The hare, however, said that he preferred to sleep outside on the grass because of the heat.

"Very well," said the buffalo, "please yourself. I shall sleep in the comfort of the hut. Be sure to shut the door firmly when you go out."

The hare could hardly control his giggles as he fastened the door so securely that it would take more than the strength of the buffalo to break it down. Then he hid behind a tree to watch the outcome of his plan.

Not long after he was rewarded by bellows and shouts coming from the hut. "The bees, the bees!" shouted the buffalo. There was a violent banging on the door. "Let me out, let me out! Oh, the bees!"

For no sooner had the buffalo unrolled his sleeping mat than the angry bees had set upon him, stinging him all over his head and body.

Eventually the lion too heard the screams. As he broke down the door to rescue his friend, the buffalo rushed out with a swarm of bees buzzing about him. The lion was also attacked as they raced into the shadows of the night.

"What happened, my friend?" asked the lion when at last they had managed to escape from the fury of the bees.

"It was the hare's doing," whimpered the buffalo. "The wicked creature rolled up the bees in my sleeping mat. The scoundrel! I'll punish him for this. Where is he?"

But the hare was far, far away by that time, and he took very great care to give the buffalo a wide berth from then on!

The Wolf Queen

An unusual story of Malay-Indian provenance, as recounted by the Malay people of the Cape and recorded by Dr I. D. du Plessis, who dedicated many years of his life to the preservation of this unique cultural heritage. The illustrator is Natalie Hinrichsen.

AN OLD SULTAN WHO HAD RULED his land for many years had to ride through a forest one day. It was a beautiful summer's day and the birds were singing in every tree, but the sultan didn't hear them. His thoughts were with his wife, who had died a few months earlier and over whom he was still grieving. His people wanted another sultana, but not one of the ladies of the court appealed to him.

It was hot and the sultan was thirsty. When he came to a woodcutter's hut in the forest, he sent one of his attendants to knock at the door and ask for water.

A beautiful girl opened the door. She was so beautiful that the soldier who had knocked at the door couldn't believe his eyes. He completely forgot why he had knocked at the door in the first place.

Impatiently the sultan sent for him. "Why are you standing there dawdling? Don't the people have water for us to drink?"

"Forgive me, my Lord," said the soldier. "I did want to ask, but the girl who opened the door is so beautiful that I was dumbstruck."

The sultan went to see for himself, and indeed, he had never seen such a delightful being before. He drank some water, thanked her politely and went on his way.

But he could not forget the girl's face.

The following day he went to ask for water again, and the third day once more.

Then the girl began to feel afraid, because she could see that the sultan was in love with her and intended to make her his sultana.

Now one would think that any girl would be only too happy to become a sultana, but this simple woodcutter's daughter was already in love and wanted no other suitor than the handsome young wazir to whom her heart belonged.

After the third visit the sultan stayed away for a few

days. The girl was happy, because she thought that he had decided to choose another wife. But just as she was beginning to relax, the sultan came riding up one day on a pitch-black horse with a blood-red saddle-cloth and copper bells that tinkled as the horse trotted along.

"Amina," he said, "I want you to be my sultana. Will you agree to be my wife?"

But she quickly made a plan to create a delay. "I don't have any nice clothes. First you must bring me a silver dress."

"Fine," said the sultan.

Then she ran to the house of the wazir to ask for his advice, but he wasn't there.

The next day, the sultan arrived on a snow-white horse with a silver saddle-cloth and silver bells that tinkled as the horse trotted along.

"Here is the dress," he said.

But Amina hardly looked at the silver dress. "No, that's not enough. First bring me a gold dress."

"Fine," said the sultan.

Then she ran to the house of the wazir to ask for his advice, but he wasn't there.

The next day, the sultan came riding on a chestnut horse with a golden saddle-cloth and gold bells that tinkled as the horse trotted along.

"Here is the dress," he said.

But Amina hardly looked at the golden dress. "No, that's not enough. First bring me a dress made of diamonds."

Now the sultan began to get impatient, but Amina smiled so prettily that he promised to do as she had asked.

When he had left, she ran to the house of the wazir once again. This time he was there, and Amina told him everything and asked for his advice.

"There is a way out," the wazir said when she had finished. "Take this magic ring and always wear it on the middle finger of your left hand. Also take this wolf's pelt. If the sultan comes tomorrow and he wants to take you to the palace, go to your bedroom, pull the pelt over your shoulders, rub the ring and then sing the following words:

Nasoedindi
Ja terima batoeng.
Bira, bira,
Nokiaoela,
Bira, bira,
Nokiaoela.

The following afternoon the sultan came riding on a dappled horse with a saddle-cloth studded with diamonds and crystal bells that tinkled as the horse trotted along.

"Here is the dress," he said.

This time Amina admired the dress and asked the sultan to come inside. "Wait here in the sitting-room," she said. "I want to go and put it on."

But instead of the dress, she pulled the wolf's pelt over her shoulders, rubbed the ring and sang the words which the wazir had taught her.

The sultan waited for a long time, but when Amina had still not appeared after half an hour he knocked at the door of her bedroom. When there was no reply, he opened the door.

On the bed lay a wolf, with its head on its paws and flashing eyes that watched the sultan's every move.

When the sultan gripped his sword, the wolf jumped out of the window.

Of Amina there was no trace.

With a heavy heart the sultan returned to the palace, because he knew now that he would never take Amina back there as his bride.

But Amina would not get off so lightly. When she rubbed the ring to take on her human form again, she had forgotten the words of the song. She wandered around in the wolf's pelt, aimless and afraid, till a group of hunters came across her.

"Look, it's a tame wolf," said one of the hunters as Amina stood so frozen with fear that she couldn't run away.

They caught her and put her in a cage on the estate of the wazir. But he was ill in bed and knew nothing about the matter.

That afternoon, just before sunset, a couple of the hunters brought some water and a piece of meat for the wolf, but it didn't want to eat a thing.

"It will die of hunger," said the one.

"Oh, well, it won't be our fault," said the other. "There is more than enough food here. Are you going to dance at the house of the wazir's brother tonight?"

"Yes."

When Amina heard this, she was filled with a burning desire to attend the dance. She thought and thought, but only when the sun went down did she suddenly remember the words of the song. She rubbed the ring, and when she had returned to her human form, she ran to her father's house in the forest and put on the silver dress.

That evening she was the most beautiful woman in the hall. Everyone was talking about the unknown sultan's daughter, but no one could say where she had come from.

Amina danced with the brother of the wazir but nowhere could she see the man she loved.

"Where is your brother then?" she asked at last.

"My brother is ill, but he will surely be here tomorrow evening," he replied.

Then Amina slipped out of the hall, went home and exchanged her silver dress for the wolf's pelt, rubbed the ring and sang the song. After that, she went back to lie in the wolf's cage.

When the sun rose, she had forgotten the song once again.

The next evening even more guests arrived, the food was more tasty, and the music more lively. Of all the pretty women, the unknown poeteri with her golden dress was the most beautiful. But once more the wazir wasn't there.

When the hunters came to the cage the next morning, the wolf was sitting in a corner, as usual.

That evening, the dancing reached its climax. All the guests wore their best clothes, the lights sparkled as never before, two orchestras took it in turns to play music and the guests danced non-stop.

The most beautiful of all was the poeteri in the diamond-studded dress.

But the wazir wasn't there. At the crack of dawn, Amina went to exchange the diamond-studded dress for the wolf's pelt and crept into the cage.

That day the wazir got out of bed, and while walking around the garden, he came across the cage.

"And now? What is this?" he asked one of the hunters who was standing there.

The hunter told him how they had caught the wolf in the countryside.

Then the brother of the wazir arrived and he told him about the beautiful poeteri who had attended the dance.

"Could it have been the woodcutter's daughter?" wondered the wazir, and he went to stand in front of the wolf's cage. "Amina!" he called.

The wolf ran this way and that, but couldn't say a word because it was still early in the afternoon and Amina would only remember the words of the song after sunset.

But the wazir knew that it was Amina. He opened the door of the cage, grabbed the wolf by the throat and ordered his guards to kill it at once.

Then Amina appeared, more beautiful than ever before, and the wazir embraced her and took her to his home. Later the wazir became a sultan and he always called his wife "The Wolf Queen".

Translator: MARGUERITE GORDON

Van Hunks and the Devil

This is another version of the well-known tale about Table Mountain's white tablecloth. This story dates from the early years when the Cape of Storms was still circumnavigated by sailing ships and the settlement at the Cape was a Dutch colony. It is retold here by ANNARI VAN DER MERWE, and DIEK GROBLER is the illustrator.

ONCE, IN THE DAYS WHEN there was only a handful of houses huddling in the shadow of Table Mountain, a great sailing ship dropped anchor in Table Bay. Soon the quay was packed with people: fish sellers, fruit vendors, farmers and wealthy citizens in their finery; even the man who played the bugle at the Cape Castle was there. Everyone was curious, because such a big ship always brought something interesting to see and something interesting to talk about.

The passengers streamed off the ship the moment the gangplank was lowered. They were weaving and staggering a little, because after all their weeks at sea, they weren't used to solid land any more. The throng at the harbour was about to turn away in disappointment, sad that this time there was nothing of any great interest on board, when a tall man with a broad, muscular chest appeared on deck. A murmur rippled through the crowd. "It's Van Hunks!" someone gasped.

"But look at him now!" said someone else. "When last we saw him he was a lowly sailor. And now? Look at those expensive clothes! Look at that fine satin waistcoat! Who would have thought that?"

Van Hunks stood to one side while porters carried his baggage to the dock: three enormous suitcases and a small wooden chest that he kept within arm's reach at all times. He never took his eye off that chest. Jamming his hat firmly on his head, the big seaman stalked through the crowd of people, looking neither right nor left as he passed.

"The rumours must be true," said someone in the crowd. "He has become a pirate. What else could be in that chest but looted treasure?"

Van Hunks vanished into the crowd on the Parade, with the porters scuttling close behind him. But Van Hunks did not stop there; he walked quickly and purposefully in the direction of the Windy Mountain. One of the houses clinging to the slope of that mountain belonged to him.

From that day, Van Hunks was seldom seen on the streets of Cape Town – and never again near the harbour. People said he was afraid that a ship would one day bring to harbour someone he had robbed, out there on the wide blue seas. Or, they claimed, he was afraid that his old drinking buddies would try to borrow money from him, or lure him back to the grubby taverns he had once frequented.

In fact, Van Hunks preferred every day to climb up to the top of the Windy Mountain, and from there he kept a sharp eye on the bay and the harbour. He would stand for hours with his brass seaman's telescope, staring into the distance. Then he would put aside his telescope and take up his big-bowled pipe with its curved stem and blow lazy white clouds of tobacco smoke into the air.

Time passed and people began to forget about the sailor who had returned from the sea. One day, Van Hunks was sitting as usual on the top of the Windy Mountain, passing the time with his telescope and his pipe. Suddenly he realised that someone was standing behind him. Van Hunks whirled around. Standing there was a man with a black pointy hat and a small black beard at the tip of his chin. He seemed familiar – perhaps he was a drinking acquaintance from back in the days when Van Hunks spent his time in the taverns near the harbour. Van Hunks was alarmed.

But when the man said, in a very respectful tone, "Good day, Mr Van Hunks," he relaxed and began to chat. He forgot to ask the visitor his name. It had been a long time since last Van Hunks had had someone to speak to, and he just couldn't stop talking. The stranger stood and listened, his eyes narrow. When dusk fell he said good night and disappeared into the darkness, without Van Hunks noticing in which direction he had left.

A few days later Van Hunks was again on top of the Windy Mountain when the man with the black pointy hat and the little black beard unexpectedly said from behind him, "And how are you today, Mr Van Hunks?"

"Very well, thank you," Van Hunks replied, and once again he began to talk and talk, but on this occasion he began to boast as well – about how many seas he had crossed and how much treasure he had won and how many vats of rum he had brought home with him.

The stranger listened attentively. He didn't say a thing; he just nodded his head every now and again, and at dusk he once again vanished as silently as he had arrived.

It was an extremely hot day when next Van Hunks sat on top of the Windy Mountain. He just sat there smoking, too lazy even to look through his telescope. "Mr Van Hunks," said the by now familiar voice of the stranger suddenly beside him, "may I smoke a pipe with you?"

Van Hunks frowned at this, because he preferred to smoke alone. His own special pipe tobacco was particularly strong and heady, and he could blow the best smoke rings in all of the Fair Cape.

"If you like," he said reluctantly.

The stranger filled his pipe – a very attractive, slim white clay pipe – and lit up. The aroma of the tobacco was surprisingly pleasant. But soon Van Hunks noticed that a far larger cloud of smoke was cloaking the stranger than was billowing from his own pipe, and he began to inhale more deeply and exhale with more vigour.

The stranger began to do the same.

Van Hunks's broad chest began to rise and swell, rise and swell. Then he began to fill his pipe with a vengeance; fortunately, that very morning he had packed his biggest tobacco pouch.

The stranger followed suit, although Van Hunks couldn't see where his tobacco kept coming from. All he knew was that they were matching each other pipe for pipe, and the great white cloud around them was getting thicker and thicker.

"Let's swap pipes," suggested Van Hunks at last.

The stranger paused and his eyes narrowed. "All right," he said, and held out his white clay pipe to Van Hunks.

Van Hunks stuffed the big bowl of his pipe to the brim before he handed it over.

He lit the stranger's pipe and inhaled deeply. But nothing happened – he couldn't draw any smoke from the pipe. He turned angrily to the stranger. "That's cheating!" he said.

But the stranger couldn't speak. He had dragged too deeply on Van Hunks's pipe. His face turned white. Then it turned green.

"What's wrong?" asked Van Hunks, nervously smoothing his satin waistcoat.

But the man couldn't say a word. Now his face was purple, and his little narrow eyes had grown big and round. He tried to cough, but couldn't even manage a hiccup.

"Wait – let me help," said Van Hunks, and gave him a big booming slap on the back.

But instead of helping him, the slap sent the man's pointy black hat flying. Van Hunks's blood ran cold. On the stranger's head, poking from the thick black hair, were two small, pointy horns!

"You devil!" yelled Van Hunks. "You child of Satan! Take back your pipe! I'll show you a thing or two!"

The devil took his white clay pipe, and Van Hunks took back his curved pipe with the big bowl. And then they really began to smoke! Van Hunks couldn't work out how the devil drew smoke from his pipe, but soon the whole of the Windy Mountain was shrouded in smoke. Gradually the smoke spread and covered Table Mountain as well, but neither Van Hunks nor the devil was prepared to give in. Day after day they sat and smoked on top of the mountain, high above the town.

Year after year the competition continued. The Windy Mountain became known as Devil's Peak, and the handful of houses grew into a small city. The only time the pair took a break was in the winter, when it was too cold to stay sitting up there. Then the devil would go back to his home, where it was hot enough to suit a devil's taste. But no one knew where Van Hunks would retreat to in the winter, because after that first warm summer's day, back when the Cape was still Dutch, no one ever saw him up close again.

But when the white clouds come pouring down on a windy day from Devil's Peak and spill out over Table Mountain, people still look up to the mountain and say to each other, "Ah, yes, today Van Hunks and the devil are really smoking up a storm."

Translator: DARREL BRISTOW-BOVEY

Wolf and Jackal and the Barrel of Butter

South Africa's wolf-and-jackal stories have their origin in the old Flemish tales of Reynard the Fox, but over the centuries they have become so thoroughly acclimatised in South Africa that they are perceived as being part and parcel of the indigenous folklore. This retelling by PIETER W. GROBBELAAR *is illustrated by* NICOLAAS MARITZ.

WOLF AND JACKAL were walking down the road. It was a long road and they had been walking for a long time when they came upon a heavily laden wagon. It was groaning under the weight of an enormous pile of barrels. "You know, I have seen barrels like those before," said Jackal thoughtfully. "Those barrels are full of butter."

"Mmm, butter," said Wolf dreamily, his mouth watering. "I'd love to get my hands on one of them."

"Well, there is no reason why we shouldn't, my old friend," said Jackal. "Here's what we'll do: you lie down in the road, quite still, as though you're dead. Then, when the farmer loads your body onto the wagon and drives on, you quietly roll one of the barrels off the wagon. I'll hide in the long grass at the side of the road and keep an eye on things."

"Good plan," said Wolf, and off he trotted. He didn't have to lie in the road very long before the farmer came to a halt in front of him.

"Hmm," said the farmer, "I wonder if this wolf is really as dead as he seems to be." And he raised his whip and gave Wolf a couple of heavy licks. But Wolf didn't so much as twitch. "Yup," said the farmer, "he's done for, all right. I'll load him on my wagon and take him home, and later I'll skin him for his coat." So the farmer threw Wolf onto the wagon on top of the barrels of butter, and rode on.

Wolf lay there for a while without moving, in case the farmer should happen to glance back over his shoulder. Then he slowly climbed to his feet. Yeesh! That farmer knew how to use a whip! He could still feel the lash on his skin. But the moment Wolf smelt the butter, he forgot all about his aches and pains. He quickly rolled a barrel off the back of the wagon and jumped after it. Like a flash, Jackal appeared from the long grass, ever so pleased with himself. "Ah, yes, we showed that farmer a thing or two, didn't we, Wolf?" he laughed as he rolled

the barrel into the long grass. "He'll never figure out what happened to his butter."

"Come, let's open it," said Wolf. "I can't wait another moment."

"What? Eat it now?" cried Jackal in a shocked tone of voice. "We can't do that! If you eat fresh butter, you will surely die. Everyone knows that. We must wait for it to get ripe!"

So they hid the barrel of butter in the long grass and made their way home.

A few days later Wolf was sitting in the sun outside his front door. He couldn't get that barrel of butter out of his mind. Just then Jackal came strolling by. "Oi, Jackal!" called Wolf. "What do you think? Is that butter ripe yet?"

"Uh, well, Wolf, to tell you the truth, right now I have more important things on my mind than butter," said Jackal. "My wife has just had a baby, and I must take him to be baptised."

"Oh, and what are you going to call the little fellow?" asked Wolf politely.

"We're calling him . . . A Good Start!" answered Jackal, and he walked on – with some difficulty, as his stomach was bulging uncomfortably, as stomachs do when one has been filling them with butter all morning.

Wolf waited for a few days, but when he couldn't bear it any longer, he went to find Jackal. "Come on, what about that butter, Jackal?" he demanded.

"Ah, Wolf, my old friend," said Jackal in a sad tone of voice. "You aren't going to believe it, but now there is *another* baby that I must take to be baptised."

"Oh, and what will his name be?" asked Wolf with some interest, because he had already laughed long and hard over the peculiar name of Jackal's first child.

"Ummm, we're calling him . . . First Hoop," said Jackal, who that very morning had eaten so much butter

that the level had sunk down to the first hoop around the barrel.

And so it went, week after week. Wolf kept asking the same question, but Jackal was forever baptising children: Second Hoop, Third Hoop, Fourth Hoop – one after the other.

Eventually, Wolf was at his wits' end. He didn't want to think, because all he could think of was butter. He didn't want to sleep, because all he would dream of was butter.

"Don't you worry, Wolf, my old pal," said Jackal unexpectedly one day. "Tomorrow we will go and get that butter. This morning I baptised my very last child."

"That would be Seventh Hoop, I suppose?" said Wolf with a little edge to his voice. The names of Jackal's children had long since stopped striking him as amusing.

"Oh, no," said Jackal. "His name is Bottom-of-the-Barrel."

The next morning Jackal arrived, just as he had promised, and they made their way to the hidden barrel of butter.

"I tell you, Wolf, old buddy, that butter is going to taste mighty good right now," said Jackal.

"Yes," said Wolf, and he began to walk a little faster.

"It will be just about as ripe and ready as butter can be," said Jackal.

"Yes! Yes!" said Wolf, and he began to run towards the butter barrel.

"Ooh, I can already feel it melting in my mouth," said Jackal.

But Wolf couldn't even answer. His mouth was watering too much.

They arrived at the barrel and opened it up. It was empty.

"No!" gasped Jackal.

"No!" gasped Wolf.

"It was you!" said Jackal.

"It was you!" said Wolf.

Brouhaha and hullabaloo! Soon the words and the fur were flying.

"I'll slap you around the muzzle!"

"I'll pull your ears off!"

Wolf was ready to give Jackal a left hook with his fist, but Jackal quickly took a pace backwards. "Wait, wait, wait, Brother Wolf!" he said quickly. Wolf was much bigger and stronger than Jackal. If it came to a scrap, Jackal had no doubt who would come off worse. "Wait," he said again. "We are going to stand here and beat each other black and blue for nothing. Let's rather find out who the culprit is."

"It's you!" said Wolf.

"And I think it's you," said Jackal piously. "Why don't we go and lie over there in the sun, and we'll see from whose mouth the melted butter drips. Then we'll know for sure which of us is the guilty party."

"And that one will get a good and thorough hiding," said Wolf, quite certain who "that one" would be.

"Quite right," said Jackal.

They lay down in the sun. Before long, Wolf was fast asleep and snoring. Quietly, Jackal climbed to his feet, scraped the last of the butter from the bottom of the barrel and smeared it on Wolf's muzzle. Then he lay down again and went to sleep.

Later they woke up and stretched pleasantly.

"My mouth is clean," noted Jackal with some satisfaction.

"There is butter all over mine!" exclaimed Wolf in dismay.

"Well, then, I think we know what we have to do," said Jackal, breaking a nice whippy branch off a tree.

"I must have walked here in my sleep and eaten the butter," said Wolf in a dismal tone of voice, as he meekly prepared for his hiding, "because I can't remember a thing about it."

But Jackal didn't say anything. He was too busy warming up his arm to give Wolf a good and thorough hiding.

Translator: DARREL BRISTOW-BOVEY

The Cloud Princess

*In this Swazi tale, retold by PHYLLIS SAVORY, the hare is
magically transformed into a human being – an unusual event in
hare stories. The illustration is by PIET GROBLER.*

ON TWO OCCASIONS the hare had narrowly escaped being killed by the dogs belonging to the chief who owned the lands he so regularly robbed, and he was afraid that one day they would catch him.

"I must grow my own crops," he panted to himself as he lay exhausted under a bush, recovering from the latest desperate chase. He had only just managed to outwit the swiftly running dogs by doubling back when they lost sight of him for a moment.

The following morning he took his hoe and walked to the forest, where he chose a well-hidden, fertile patch of land. He cleared away the grass and then carefully dug and tilled the clods. When evening came, he returned to his little hut, worn out but satisfied.

"Tomorrow I shall plant my maize seed and pumpkin pips," he decided, as he cooked the last remaining maize cobs from his previous theft, "or one of these days those dreadful dogs will prove too swift for me."

That night he slept soundly. The next morning, after he had washed down his breakfast with some home-brewed beer, the hare left for his lands where he duly sowed his crops. When that was done to his satisfaction, he chopped down some brushwood and carefully surrounded the plot with a fence to keep out the buck.

He was fortunate in the weather, and the crops grew and prospered. As harvest time approached, the maize cobs were swelling and the pumpkins rounding favourably.

Eventually he picked the first fruits of his labour. As he sat by the fire roasting the juicy cobs, he thought how foolish he had been to risk his life so often in the chief's maize patch.

But one morning he found, to his annoyance, that maize kernels had been pecked from some of his cobs during the night. Strange bird-like footprints, such as he had never seen before, gave evidence of the theft.

"I shall set traps for these bird robbers," he said to himself, "though it is strange that they should come by night."

He went to the pastures where the chief's cattle grazed and waited until the herd boys were asleep before pulling some long, black hairs from the tail of one of the cows. Taking the hair back to his plot, he tied it into artful slip-knots, which he pegged firmly to the ground. Then he scattered earth lightly over the hair so that it would not be seen. His preparations completed, he went home, determined to catch the thieves.

He rose early, and as he neared the lands was delighted to hear the fluttering of wings. Looking over the fence, he saw that a bird was indeed trapped in one of the snares, while many of its kind circled high above in the sky, in apparent distress.

Never had he seen such a beautiful creature as his captive. Its colours were lovely as the rainbow itself, and in one wing was a pitch-black feather of great length.

"You would plunder my garden, would you?" said the hare, roughly grabbing hold of the struggling bird. "Tonight you will make a good meal for me!" And untying the knot that held it, he carried his captive home while its bird companions circled above them. He was about to kill it, but before doing so he pulled the long black feather from its wing, thinking he would place it on top of his hut as a warning to other would-be bird thieves. No sooner had he done this than the bird vanished and a beautiful maiden stood before him.

"Please give me back my magic feather," she cried tearfully.

"Oh, no," replied the hare. "You are too beautiful to escape me. If I give you back your feather, you will become a bird once more and fly back to your companions. Where is your home?"

"My home is beyond the clouds," replied the lovely maiden, "where my father rules as king. I am his only child, and those are my bird maidens circling round your hut. They are afraid to return to my parents without me. Please let me go!"

The hare had no intention of listening to her pleas and hid the magic feather in the thatch of his hut.

So the Cloud Princess was obliged to stay with him. He was kind to his beautiful prisoner. In return, she swept his hut and did all the household chores. Eventually life settled into a happy routine for them both and as the weeks went by, the Cloud Princess came to love her captor.

One day she told the hare that if he would give her back her magic feather she would change him into a human being like herself. At first he mistrusted her, thinking that she wished to play a trick on him and would fly away forever. She assured him, however, that she loved him too dearly to wish to return to her home in the clouds without him. At last he returned the feather to her.

No sooner did she hold the feather in her hand than she touched him with it, and he turned into a handsome prince, who at once asked her to marry him.

The princess readily consented, on condition that he keep their marriage secret, for should her bird maidens, who often came to circle round the hut, tell her father that she had married an earth man, he would banish her from her home in the clouds forever. Thus it was that they became man and wife, living happily together in their little hut.

The Cloud King sent many messages with her bird maidens, begging his daughter to return to her home. But as she continually refused to do so, he decided to kill the man who had won her heart.

To this end, he told her maidens to make friends with

a woodpecker and a mouse on earth. When they had done so, they were to tell the woodpecker to gather poison from the forest, and the mouse, with its ability to enter the hut unseen, to put it in her lover's food.

The two little creatures agreed to the plan and loitered near the hut to gain the confidence of the prince and his lovely wife. Soon, however, they became so fond of the prince and princess that when the time came they refused to carry out the Cloud King's bidding.

Although the Cloud Princess was very happy with her beloved husband, she eventually longed to see her people and her home once more.

"Please give me my magic feather," she begged her husband one day, "that we both may visit my people above the skies. On seeing you, it may be that they will agree to our marriage, and my father may accept you as his son."

This request her husband could not refuse, for she had been a good wife and he had grown to trust her. So he took the feather from its hiding place and she planted it in the ground, where it immediately grew upwards until it pierced the clouds above. Calling to their friends, the woodpecker and the mouse, to accompany them, they began their long climb up into the heavens. First went the prince, followed by his princess, then the woodpecker, and, last in line, the mouse.

Once they had passed through the clouds, they came to a vast wall. Where the tip of the feather rested was the mouth of a tunnel, but their way was barred by great rocks that fitted together seamlessly. "Now," said the princess, "our difficulties begin, for only my most trusted maiden knows the secret catch that moves the rock that hides the opening to my father's kingdom."

"No crevice is too small for me to find," said the mouse. "I shall feel my way around the rock until I find it." Round and round the end of the tunnel he went, trying to find a niche that would reveal the secret. But try as he would, it was such a perfect fit that he could find no place which offered a hold for his sharp little teeth.

"Let me try," said the woodpecker, "for my life has depended upon tapping tree trunks with my beak, and my ears will detect the hollow where the secret lies." *Tap, tap, tap* went the strong little beak as the woodpecker drilled at the rock, leaving not one part of the surface untapped.

"Ah," she said at last, "surely it is here, for a hollow echo sounds behind this spot." Carefully she scraped and probed with her sharp beak, eventually finding a tiny catch that was of the same grey stone as the wall and invisible to the eye. Carefully she levered and pulled until finally she loosened the catch. And when she drew it out, the rock door swung aside and they looked onto a beautiful land where green trees grew and rivers sparkled and contented cattle grazed.

"Welcome to my father's kingdom," said the princess, turning to her prince. Then she led the way into the lovely land, where they soon reached a large village with well-built huts and cattle pens.

There was much excitement among the Cloud People at the unexpected return of their princess. "But who is this man you have brought with you?" asked her father when the greetings were over.

"He is my earth friend," replied his daughter, "whom I have learned to love, and I wish him to become my husband."

"What nonsense is this?" asked the Cloud King angrily. "Cloud People have never married those who live on earth. He must return to his home at once."

The princess, however, refused to listen to her father's words, telling him that if he sent her lover away, she too would leave home forever. "His wisdom is above that of all other men," she told her father, "and you should welcome him as your son."

"Well," said the king, seeing his daughter's determination, "we shall let him stay for a while." But he thought that he would hatch a plan to kill the earth man in such a way that it would appear to be an accident. Then he gave orders for a welcoming feast to be prepared.

The mouse was fond of good food and was attracted to the kitchen by the smell of cooking. He crept in unobserved to pick up the dainties that fell to the floor. But his eyes and ears were sharp, and he heard the chief cook discussing the king's orders to poison the earth man. He watched carefully, and after all the platters of choice food had been prepared, he saw one being set aside. Then the king's head magician came in to sprinkle a white powder over it.

The mouse lost no time in running to the prince. Climbing onto his shoulder, he whispered, "Your life is in danger! Eat no food today." Then he told him all that he had seen and heard in the royal kitchen. Thus the prince was saved.

The king was angry that his plan had failed, so he summoned his head magician. To ensure that no one would overhear the wicked plan, the two discussed it under the big council tree.

"This time," said the king, "you must conjure up a mighty hailstorm on the big plain that stretches to the horizon between my kingdom and the neighbouring territory. I shall send the princess's lover on an errand across the plain, where the hail will kill him."

Unbeknown to the king, the woodpecker was sunning herself high in the branches of the tree, and her sharp ears overheard the conversation, so she made some plans of her own.

The following morning, the king sent for the prince. "I want you to take a message," he said, "to my neighbour far across the big plain that separates our kingdoms. If you are to live with us, it is wise for you to know the people around us."

The next morning the prince left on his journey. But when he was halfway across the plain, far from shelter of any kind, black clouds began to gather in the sky. Fierce lightning flashed and thunder rolled.

"I might be killed," he thought, and soon the hail fell in huge chunks of jagged ice. But before it could touch his head, the woodpecker, who had followed him unseen, covered him with her magic wings. Telling him to lie down, she protected him from the danger from above.

When the storm had passed, he stood up in a daze. There was nothing but desolation as far as the eye could see. But although the hail lay deep upon the ground, no harm had come to the prince.

The king's anger when the prince returned unscathed can be imagined. He called in all his magicians. "We must arrange a hunt in the prince's honour," they finally decided. "There will be many hunters with their bows and arrows, and who will know whose arrow killed him?"

Again the woodpecker was sitting in the tree top and heard the wicked plan. She flew swiftly to the head magician's hut, where she prepared a magic charm. She told the prince to wear it concealed around his neck. This, she assured him, would turn the arrows away from his body.

On the day of the hunt, many of the hunters tried to

gain the king's reward by killing the prince. Yet, although their aim was true, their arrows repeatedly fell harmlessly to the ground without having met their mark. Again the prince returned unharmed.

"My sweet one," he said to the Cloud Princess that night, "your father will not rest until he has killed me. It is time for me to return to my home on earth."

"Life without you, my husband, would be as nothing to me," she told him. "I shall return with you."

So in the dead of night, when all were fast asleep, the prince, the princess, the woodpecker and the mouse stole quietly to the door that led from the clouds. As the princess threw the magic feather down to the earth far below, it landed at the door of the prince's little hut. Then they all climbed down to leave the land of the Cloud People forever.

"Wish what you will," said the woodpecker to the prince, "and your magic charm will provide it."

"My greatest wish of all is for a home befitting my wife."

At once a beautiful village appeared before them, peopled with subjects who saluted him as their king. Soft-eyed cattle grazed knee-deep in green pastures, and a kind and wrinkled old woman led a party of maidens to guide the princess to her royal hut.

The prince's next wish was for the mouse and the woodpecker to become human beings, which took place in a twinkling. Then a feast was ordered to celebrate the marriage of the prince and his Cloud Princess. The mouse became the chief councillor, and the four friends lived to a ripe and happy old age, ruling their people wisely and well.

The Guardian of the Pool

*A story from Central Africa in which the healing abilities of the snake are portrayed —
another familiar theme in the folklore of Africa. The story is retold here by* DIANA PITCHER,
who has given it a Zululand setting. The illustrator is TAMSIN HINRICHSEN.

IN A LAND far away there is a great lake. At one end of the lake the water finds a small opening and slithers through it to gurgle its way down towards the plains. Through narrow, rock-strewn ravines, over cliffs, through the brown earth and green grasses it flows, until it is hemmed in by three large rocks.

The river whirls round and round, trying to find a way out; round and round, faster and faster, until it makes a great whirlpool that sucks in the red and gold leaves that fall from the umsasa trees, the gnats that dart across the water and the butterflies that flutter over the sweet-scented white flowers of the pondweed growing at the water's edge.

At the bottom of the whirlpool lies a great silver water python, coil upon glittering coil of him, his snake eyes blinking at the shafts of sunlight striking the water, his tongue flickering — a beautiful, terrible, silver water python who is the guardian of the pool.

But this is no ordinary python, for in the touch of his cold, wet skin lies healing: healing for all the illnesses and pains of men and women, healing for all who are brave enough to visit him in his home at the bottom of the pool.

Ngosa sat beside the pool and watched the angry water swirl about. The sun shone on her smooth brown skin and warmed her trembling body. Her mother was ill, very ill. Ngosa knew her mother would die unless she brought help. But to step down into those angry waters, to touch the silver python, to look into his black snake eyes, to draw near to that flickering tongue . . . In spite of the heat, Ngosa shivered. She was afraid.

From beneath the water Python gazed up at Ngosa and saw that she was beautiful, knew that she feared him and longed to comfort her.

Ngosa heard a cry behind her and turned to see her younger sister hurrying across the fields.

"Ngosa! Ngosa!" she called. "Make haste, for our mother is surely dying."

Then Ngosa remembered many things – how her mother had soothed her and sat beside her singing lullabies all the night after Crocodile had nearly drawn her into the water; how her mother had walked many miles to find the red radish roots to cure the terrible pain when Scorpion had stung her; how her mother had beaten off the hairy baboon-monster that had tried to steal her baby brother; how her mother had secretly shared her own portion of maize porridge with the children when the great drought had come upon them and men were starving.

Ngosa stepped into the raging whirlpool.

Python's tongue flickered once before her and was still. The black snake eyes closed. She stretched out her hand and stroked his cool, wet skin. Then, flailing the water with her arms and legs, she rose to the surface of the pool and raced across the fields to touch her mother with the python's healing touch.

That night, as a full moon rose blood red above the mountains, Python uncoiled his silver body and slowly rose to the top of the pool. Out of the water stepped a young man. His handsome head, held high, was covered in tight black curls. His brown eyes were fearless. His arms and legs were strong. Surely this was a chief's son. As the first man had once done, he looked about him and saw that the earth was good.

Striding across the fields, he came to the semi-circle of huts. In the enclosure the cattle quietly chewed the cud, their black and white skins soft and silky in the moonlight. A nanny-goat nuzzled her kid.

"Ngosa," he called softly. "Ngosa, your courage has saved me. When the water-witch cast her snake-spell upon me, I sank to the bottom of the pool. Forever, by day, I must continue to guard the whirlpool. But now, because of your courage, by night I may assume my human form. By night I may reveal myself to those who are brave and beautiful. You are surely brave to have visited me in my python form, and I can see that you are beautiful. Come."

As Ngosa stepped from her hut, the chief's son slipped round her neck a necklace of milky blue and green moonstones, strung on a thread of silver moonlight.

Now Ngosa spends her days at the whirlpool's edge, playing sweet music on her ugubhu, for pythons love to hear the music of human beings.

And at night she slips her moonstone necklace around her neck and waits for the chief's son to rise from the water.

The Sultan's Daughter

Tales about riddles that first have to be solved before someone's heart's desire can be fulfilled are found the world over.
In this Malay-Indian story, recorded in the Malay quarter of the Cape and retold by DR I.D. DU PLESSIS, the chief
protagonist must also solve three riddles before he gets his reward. The illustration is by ROBERT HICHENS.

SULTAN MAHMOED had only one son, Ali. Mahmoed was old and felt that he wouldn't live much longer. So he called Ali and said, "My son, before I die, I want you to prove that you have the wisdom and the courage to be my successor. Take this money and your horse and go out into the world. But don't stay away for longer than a year, because I am getting old and I want to see you again before I die."

Ali had hardly left his father's country when his horse fell ill, and after a few days it died. Ali had to continue on foot but he didn't mind. He wandered through the unknown land and saw the beauty of the world around him, with its forests and trees and all the creatures of the wild, and he was happy because he was young and full of zest for life.

One afternoon, the weather suddenly turned foul and Ali went to look for shelter in a house that was surrounded by trees. When he got closer he saw that it was a mosque, but there was no one else there. Ali decided to spend the night there because the weather was too unpleasant for him to continue his journey.

During the night he was woken by muted blows so powerful that he felt the floor beneath him shudder. He quietly got up and tried to make out what was happening, but it was so dark that he couldn't see a thing. The thudding continued and every now and then he heard people whispering close by.

When it grew light, he saw that two men were digging up the floor of the mosque with pickaxes. As he watched them, they dragged out a skeleton from under the floor tiles. This was sacrilege! Ali couldn't contain his rage. Brandishing his sword, he rushed towards them.

"Stop your evil deed," he shouted, "or I'll chop off your heads!"

When the grave-robbers saw that he was alone they grew defiant.

"And what business is it of yours?" they asked.

"I am Ali, son of Sultan Mahmoed, and I will not allow such sacrilege even though I am in a foreign land!"

The men addressed him more politely.

"It may be sacrilege, but we are only taking revenge for what this man did to us: he owed us a large sum of money and died before he had paid it back."

"Is that not punishment enough? Do you think he is at peace in the world of the spirits when he thinks about that money?"

"No, perhaps not, but that doesn't give us our money back," one of the men said grumpily. "That loan made us poor and now he must be punished."

"By taking revenge in this way you are harming your own souls," said Ali. "But tell me, how much did the poor man owe you?"

"Five hundred coins."

"If I pay you on his behalf, you must promise me to lay his bones carefully back in the grave and to seal it up again."

The creditors were only too pleased to agree. But when Ali had handed them the correct amount there was nothing left in his purse.

The next day Ali was walking through the countryside singing aloud: his horse was dead and his purse was empty, but his heart was full because he had done the dead man a favour.

While he was still walking along like this, a stranger caught up with him from the rear. "That's strange," thought Ali. "I looked back just now, and there was no one on the road."

But the man had a friendly face and Ali liked him on sight.

"Asalaam-u-alaikum!" said the stranger.

"Wa-alaikum salaam!" replied Ali.

"May I join you?" asked the stranger.

"Of course. Where are you going?"

"Nowhere special. My name is Radjab and I would like to travel with you for a while."

They walked on together until they came to a pitch-black mountain.

"Look how black the mountain is!" Ali exclaimed. "Do you think it's bad weather?"

"No," said Radjab, "that's just the colour of the mountain. It's a strange mountain, this one. See that you never wander near it on your own. They call it the Witch's House."

As they walked past the mountain, they came across a woman carrying a load of wood. As she drew close to them, she stumbled over a stone and twisted her knee, with the result that she couldn't walk any further.

"Poor woman," said Ali. "What can we do to help her?"

Radjab dug his hand into his pocket. "I have just the right kind of ointment for her."

He rubbed it onto the woman's knee and immediately she was better.

"What can I do to express my gratitude?" the woman said.

"It won't cost you anything," said Radjab, "but if you like, I'll take those two fronds of bracken that you are carrying."

The woman was only too happy to give the bracken to him. Then she picked up her bundle of wood, said goodbye to the two friends and went on her way.

"What do you want to do with the bracken?" asked Ali.

"It may come in handy," answered Radjab.

At sunset they came to an inn where they decided to spend the night. After supper they were sitting at the door of the inn, enjoying the cool mountain air, when a fakir came up and started to entertain the guests with his magic tricks. He was an exceptional fakir, because he could make his wooden puppets walk without using any strings.

While the guests were still sitting and watching, a dog pounced on one of the puppets and tore the head from the body. The magician was furious, because he could not fix the magic doll. He wanted to strike the dog with his sword, but Radjab intervened and said, "Leave the dog; it doesn't know any better. Look, I will fix the doll in such a way that it will not only be able to walk again but it will also be able to talk."

Radjab took out his little jar of ointment, rubbed it onto the doll's neck and head and stuck them together. And indeed, the doll started walking around and talking so much that even the fakir felt a little afraid!

"What must I give you for this?" the fakir asked Radjab.

"It won't cost you anything," said Radjab, "but if you want to give me that sword, I would be happy to take it."

"What do you want to do with the sword?" asked Ali when they set out again the following morning.

"It may come in handy," replied Radjab.

In the distance there appeared the minarets of a great city, and Radjab suggested that they visit it. Just as they came to the gate in the city wall, Ali heard a crystal-clear song in the air. He looked up and saw a snow-white bird soaring above them.

"Listen how beautifully that bird is singing," he said.

"Yes, that's a good bird. It's singing a poedji, a sacred song," answered Radjab.

The words had hardly left his mouth when the bird fell down dead at their feet. Radjab took the sword from its sheath, cut off the bird's wings and put them in his bag.

"What do you want to do with the bird's wings?" asked Ali.

"They may come in handy," replied Radjab.

A colourful crowd jostled in the marketplace, bowing before a beautiful young princess who was riding through the masses on a chestnut stallion. Everyone remarked on her beauty.

"Who is that woman on the horse?" Ali asked one of the bystanders.

"That's the poeteri, the daughter of the sultan. She is the most beautiful woman in the country, but also the most cruel. Any man who wants to marry her must first solve a riddle which she poses. If he cannot guess the answer, he is put to death."

"I like the poeteri," Ali said to Radjab. "She may be cruel, but she has stolen my heart. Tomorrow I am going to the palace to see if I can solve her riddle!"

"All right," said Radjab, "but then let us go to bed early tonight. Your mind must be sharp if you want to solve the poeteri's riddle."

Before they went to sleep, Radjab rubbed a little of his ointment on Ali's forehead. "It will make you sleep well," he said.

Ali's head had hardly touched the pillow before he was fast asleep. Just before midnight, Radjab got up, strapped the wings of the bird to his shoulders, took the bracken twigs in his right hand and flew out of the window to the sultan's palace, where he landed in the garden and waited under a tree.

When the clock struck midnight, the poeteri came flying through her window on golden wings. She flew straight to a cave in the Witch's House, without noticing that Radjab was flying behind her. As they flew, Radjab struck her with the bracken, but she didn't look round because she thought the blows were raindrops falling on her back.

At the door to the cave, the poeteri knocked *rat-a-tat-tat* and it opened. The witch was sitting in front of a

fire and the most gruesome creatures were crawling around her and over her.

"What is your wish?" asked the witch.

"It's been a long time since someone came to solve my riddle. They all want to come and guess but they are afraid of death. Now I know it won't be long before someone comes again and I'm afraid that the answer to the old riddle may have slipped out. Who knows, perhaps I have talked in my sleep."

"All right," said the witch. "If someone comes, you must tell him to guess what you are thinking about."

"Yes, but what shall I think about then?"

"Think of your gloves."

When the poeteri flew back, Radjab was hot on her heels, and again he lashed her with the bracken. Then he went back to sleep next to Ali till the sun came up.

"If the poeteri asks you what she is thinking about, say she is thinking about her gloves," Radjab said to Ali as he was getting ready to go to the palace.

When the poeteri saw what an attractive young man had come to solve the riddle, she liked him immediately and almost wished that he would get it right. But when he actually did, she jumped up angrily and said, "No, you must come and guess again. You can't have me that easily!"

That evening Radjab put Ali into a deep sleep again and at midnight he flew to the palace. This time he struck the poeteri till the lashes showed across her shoulders, but she carried on flying till she came to the cave.

"And how did it go with the guessing?" asked the witch.

"He guessed the right answer."

"Is that so?" exclaimed the witch. "You must be care-

ful that that young man doesn't become your husband!"

"Give me a riddle that he won't be able to solve."

The witch said, "Ask him again to guess what you are thinking about and then think of the golden crown on your head."

The poeteri flew home quickly, but Radjab was right behind her and flogged her with the bracken.

The next morning Radjab said to Ali, "If the poeteri asks you what she is thinking about, then you must answer, 'About the golden crown that is on your head.'"

The poeteri was sitting very proudly on a throne next to her father. "This time," she thought, "at least he won't guess the right answer." But when she heard the correct answer she was very angry.

"You must come again," she said. "It can't be so easy."

"The condition was that I had to guess only once," said Ali, "but so as not to disappoint you, poeteri, I will come again."

That night Radjab followed the poeteri once more and thrashed her till her shoulders were bleeding and she could hardly fly any further.

"Now you must give me a riddle that no one on earth will be able to guess," she said to the witch.

"All right," said the witch. "Think about my head. He will never guess that."

The poeteri flew back and collapsed in her room, so thoroughly had Radjab tackled her with the bracken. "I am never flying to that creature again," she said, and she tore the golden wings to shreds.

But Radjab flew back to the Witch's House and knocked *rat-a-tat-tat* at the door to the cave.

"Come in!" called the witch from inside the cave, but when no one entered she stuck her head out of the door.

Radjab was ready for her. With one blow of his sword he chopped off her head and stuck it in his bag. Then he flew back and went to sleep next to Ali.

"Take my bag with you," he said to Ali the next morning. "When the poeteri asks you what she is thinking about, take out what is in the bag and show it to her."

That morning the poeteri sat uneasily next to her father. Her shoulders were very sore and she was tired of all the guessing.

"What am I thinking about?" she asked Ali.

Ali said nothing, and the executioner lifted his axe and looked at the poeteri. But before she could give the sign, Ali took the witch's head out of the bag and showed it to her. With a cry of joy, the poeteri fell into his arms.

"Now you don't have to make any more guesses. I will marry you!"

Great was the joy of the sultan and his subjects, and the wedding was arranged immediately. But when Ali asked Radjab to be the best man, he smiled and shook his head.

"By the time that you are living with the poeteri in the palace, I will be far away from here in my own resting place," he said. "Now that I have settled my debt, you may also know who I am."

"But who are you then, and what is the debt you are talking about?" asked Ali in amazement.

"I am the spirit of the man whose bones you protected from being disturbed. Farewell, my friend. I may not stay with you any longer."

Before Ali could say another word, Radjab had vanished.

Then Ali went back to his father and told him everything that had happened.

Sultan Mahmoed travelled back with him to the land of the poeteri and attended the wedding. Then he handed his throne over to Ali and died a peaceful death.

Translator: MARGUERITE GORDON

The Ring of the King

This free-wheeling tale by children's book specialist JAY HEALE
carries with it echoes of mythical African kingdoms such as the magnificent,
fabulous Monomotapa. The illustration is by NEELS BRITZ.

ONCE THERE WAS A KING – a king with a ring. In that ring lay the secret of his power and greatness.

The ring was made of gold brought up the River Nile, inlaid with silver brought up the River Congo, and topped with diamonds brought up the River Zambezi – so the story went, though exactly where it had come from, no one was sure. The ring was so powerful that whoever wore it was protected from all mortal danger. That meant that no matter how many people came charging round the corner waving spears and axes or shooting arrows, the king could never get hurt – provided, of course, that he was wearing the ring.

So the king wore the ring at all times – while passing judgement in his court, while eating stupendous feasts that lasted all day, while being carried on a special sort of bed covered with ostrich feathers through the streets of his city, and even while sleeping in the royal bedchamber at night.

The king wore the magic ring every hour of every day, except when he went for his ceremonial bath. On these occasions, the king was carried to the crystal-clear pool beside the waterfall. There all his servants and his children and his many wives bowed low to him, and then backed away out of sight.

Once they had left, the king would take off his crown of gold and ivory and peacock feathers, his cloak of gold and silk and precious stones, his sandals of ebony and rhinoceros hide, and his robe of the purest white linen. And then he would take off his ring and hide it in a place so secret and well concealed that neither his servants, nor his children, nor even his many wives could make the slightest guess as to where it was. And as soon as he had finished his royal bath, the ring was the first thing the king put on again, before he allowed anyone to come anywhere near him. He treasured the ring, because it made him the most powerful king in Africa.

THE RING OF THE KING 103

But the day arrived when he stepped, dripping, out of his ceremonial bath into the warm sun, to find that the ring was not there. At first with amazement and then with fear, the king searched his secret hiding place and all around it. The ring was gone. Somebody – somebody among all his servants and his children and his many wives – must have discovered the hiding place and dared to take the ring.

The king was furious. But he was also afraid. If he offered great rewards for finding the ring, then everyone would know that he no longer had it. They would know that he was no longer protected from harm. They would know that he was no longer the most powerful king in Africa.

For days the king sat and worried. He paced up and down his private chamber; he sat for hours staring at the ground or at the sky; he couldn't sleep. All his wives shook their heads in sorrow, and his children kept well away. It was his favourite wife who persuaded him to tell her what was wrong. Immediately she went to the house of the wisest of all the diviners, a man called Zafusa.

With wild eyes and bracelets jangling on his arms, Zafusa sprang into the courtyard where the king was sitting. Plumes of feathers danced and waved in his head-dress, and strips of furry skin dangled from his waist. He looked like a feathered leopard with a hundred tails. He listened silently while the king told him about the stolen ring.

Then Zafusa opened one of the leather pouches that hung from his beaded belt and took out the set of bones that he used to find the answers to difficult questions. Smoothing a circle in the sand, Zafusa held the bones towards the sky, gave a sharp cry and then dropped them. Carefully, he examined the pattern in which they lay. Then Zafusa straightened up and looked at the king.

"Your ring will be found, Your Majesty," he said. "The thief is close to us."

"Who is it?" demanded the king.

Zafusa shook his head. "You shall see. You will not need magic. Send for your woodcutters."

The king did so at once, and Zafusa explained to them what was needed. At dawn on the next day, all those who could possibly have had the slightest chance to steal the ring were gathered in the great square in front of the palace.

The king appeared at the top of the steps leading down from the front door and stood there, staring silently at the bowing people. Then he clapped his hands and soldiers appeared all round the square, ready and armed with sharpened spears so that no one could escape. Through a small archway appeared Zafusa, all the more terrible now with white circles around each eye and strange dark designs on his body. After him came the woodcutters with great numbers of straight wooden sticks. They heaped the sticks in the centre of the square.

Zafusa danced around the sticks, chanting in a language nobody had heard before, and it was clear to even the smallest child that he was casting a spell on the sticks. Finally, at the king's command, everyone in the square was given one stick.

"Take care!" thundered Zafusa. "These sticks are full of power. Do not lose them. Have them with you all through today. Bring them back here at dawn tomorrow. As the sun rises, we shall see what we shall see."

Sticks of power! All the people were amazed – the sticks looked so ordinary. They compared sticks with each other – they all looked just the same. A few were a little thicker or thinner, but they were all the same length. In fact, they were all *exactly* the same length. How curious!

The Clever Snake Charmer

From Morocco comes this entertaining story about a clever snake charmer who knows how to push his luck. Once again there are three riddles that have to be answered. JEAN FULLALOVE *is the illustrator.*

SULTAN JADI – may blessings be upon him – was very bored in his palace. So he called for his fiddler, Mohammed. For a few days he took pleasure in listening to the fiddler, and he even started laughing and cracking jokes again. But it was not long before he tired of the fiddler and had the unlucky fellow's head chopped off.

Then he called for Joseph, his harp-player. But it was not long before the music of the harp was just a scratching in his ears and he had the harpist's head chopped off too.

Many more men came to entertain the sultan and cheer him up, but each time he was content only for a short while. Then he would become restless and angry and call for his soldiers to drag them away and have them beheaded.

The situation grew so bad that everyone in the city sat and trembled. Each one wondered if he would be the next to be called to the sultan's palace, only to die by the sword a few days later. Soon everyone fled: the storytellers, the musicians, the dancers, the jugglers. Everyone left the city where the powerful sultan lived.

But one morning Selham the snake charmer arrived at the palace and bravely announced that he would like a chance to entertain the sultan. They brought him to the sultan and the sultan looked at him with interest, this man who played his flute with the snakes that slithered out of his sack and wound themselves around his legs and neck.

But it was not too long before the sultan was once more bored and irritable. He felt no further inclination to watch the flute-player with his snakes. That evening, when Selham picked up his flute and his snakes to leave, the sultan said, "My friend, I've had enough of your flute-playing and your snakes. I will command my servant to cut off your head with the sword."

"My Lord," said Selham, "as you say, so it must be.

But give me one chance. If you give me a chance, it will be well worth your while."

"Very well," said the sultan. "I will do it gladly. But you must earn your chance. You will have a chance if tomorrow when you arrive here at the palace, you can be a rider and a pedestrian at the same time. This is my order. Those who do not obey my orders perish by the sword."

Selham bowed and departed. Early the next morning the sultan stood on the terrace before his palace to watch the snake charmer's arrival. When the palace gates opened, the sultan's eyes nearly popped out of his head and he couldn't utter a word. There was Selham coming through the gates on the back of the smallest donkey the sultan had ever seen. The donkey was so small that Selham's feet touched the ground on both sides. As he came towards the sultan he was riding the donkey, but at the same time he was walking.

"Very well," said the sultan. "You have done what you had to do. But you have not quite finished. If you do not wish me to hand you over to the man with the sword, you must answer three questions. Here is the first: How many stars are there in the heavens?"

"My Lord," answered the snake charmer, "there are just as many stars in the heavens as there are hairs on my donkey, excluding those on his tail. You can count them for yourself."

"Very well," said the sultan. "Now tell me: On what part of the earth are we?"

"In the middle."

The sultan laughed and asked, "How many hairs are there in my beard?"

"Just as many as on the tail of my donkey. Cut off your beard and I will cut off my donkey's tail. Then we can count together."

Finally the sultan replied, "No, you are too clever. There are no questions that you cannot answer."

He beckoned to one of his courtiers and sent him to fetch something. The man came back and pressed a sack of gold into Selham's hands.

The snake charmer bowed deeply to the sultan and walked outside to his little donkey.

Once more the sultan went onto his terrace to watch the clever man riding – but at the same time walking – out of the gates of his palace. Yes, Selham was leaving on the smallest donkey that the sultan had ever seen.

Translator: MARGARET AUERBACH

Asmodeus and the Bottler of Djinns

A latter-day tale by ALEX D'ANGELO *about the olden-days Cape, in which
the reader meets the luckless Asmodeus, a junior fiend who has been despatched from Hell
to set up a regional office at the Cape. The illustrator is* GEOFFREY WALTON.

"I WANT TO GET RID OF ASMODEUS," said the Governor of the Cape to the Sheikh. "He's far too much of a problem walking around on the loose."

The Sheikh stroked his beard and smiled.

"Then you are speaking to the right man," he said. "I have bottled many imps and djinns and spirits of the desert in my time, and one more should not be too difficult."

The Governor was impressed. Everyone knows stories of fishermen opening magic bottles full of djinns – but when you think of it, letting the spirits out is the easy part; the tricky bit is getting them in.

The Governor reached an agreement with the Sheikh, who proceeded to have a special bottle made. It was of very thick green glass and was bound with copper plating, with gaps here and there where the glass showed through. The Sheikh was not a hard-hearted man. He didn't mind leaving Asmodeus a window or two. Besides, he thought it a good idea to let potential openers of the bottle look inside it first so they could see what they were going to get.

Once the bottle was ready, the Sheikh held its neck in hot water so that it expanded just enough for him to drop a cheap copper ring inside. When the bottle cooled down the neck contracted to its normal size and the ring could not be shaken out.

The Sheikh tested this by walking round and round on the slopes of Devil's Peak, trying to shake the ring out and wailing to himself.

Rattle-rattle-rattle went the ring in its bottle. The Sheikh wailed and rattled all morning and well into the afternoon, until Asmodeus grew fed up at the noise and popped out of the ground to complain.

"Right! That's enough!" he snarled. "What's all this sheikh-rattle-and-roll racket about then, eh?"

The Sheikh flung himself down in abasement.

"Oh, Devil!" he began. "I have a bottle that contains a magic ring. If only I could get it out, all my troubles would be over. But look, it will not come out!"

Asmodeus's bat-winged ears fanned out at the mention of a magic ring. He was thinking about how easily he could run the Cape Hell with the help of a magic ring. "No more shovelling for Asmodeus," he was thinking. "No more stoking the boilers in the middle of the night. A legion of imps could do it for me!"

"Gimme that!" snapped Asmodeus, snatching at the bottle. "Er . . . I'll get it out for you," he added, for the sake of appearances.

Asmodeus held the bottle up and peered down its neck. Yes, there was a ring in there, all right.

He shook the bottle. No, the ring wouldn't come out.

Asmodeus stuck a long finger inside. *Scritch-scritch-scritch* went his talon on the glass. He hooked the ring a few times but could not manage to pull it up the neck. It kept jamming against the glass and sliding off his claw.

There was only one thing for it.

"There's only one thing for it," said Asmodeus. "I'm going in to fetch it. Once I'm holding it, I can dematerialise it and bring it out again with me. Here, hold the bottle."

Asmodeus retreated a few yards up the slope and aligned himself carefully with the bottle's mouth.

"I like a bit of a run-up for these things," he confided.

In an instant he had dwindled into a ribbon of steam and shot into the bottle. Once inside, a tiny Asmodeus materialised and, with a grunt of effort, picked up the ring.

As soon as he did this, Asmodeus knew that the ring had no magic in it whatsoever.

"There's nothing magic in this bottle!" he complained.

"Oh yes, there is!" yelled the Sheikh, fumbling a cork into the neck and sealing it tightly.

Asmodeus was furious when he realised he was trapped. He began to whizz around the bottle, bouncing off the sides and cork so that the Sheikh had to crouch down, clutching the bottle to his chest to keep it from shooting out of his grasp altogether. Little electric shocks stung the Sheikh's fingers, but he clung on until Asmodeus had calmed down.

"What now?" squeaked Asmodeus eventually. His voice buzzed tinnily like an insect's through the glass.

He wasn't resigned to his fate, exactly, but being trapped in a bottle was not a new concept to Asmodeus. Plenty of senior demons at Head Office had been caught unawares and done a century or two of bottle duty. It was said to teach one self-sufficiency.

"You have to stay in there until someone lets you out," said the Sheikh. "The rules say that you have to serve them till the end of their days when they do," he added.

"Not where I come from!" exclaimed Asmodeus in outrage. "It's 'three wishes and you're free' where I come from!"

"Well, you can negotiate your own terms with the Governor," said the Sheikh. "That's where I'm taking you."

He set off down the mountain and Asmodeus clutched wildly at the smooth sides of the bottle as he swung back and forth.

It was quite some time before he was able to speak.

"That's not a good idea!" Asmodeus squeaked. "I

know the Governor. He'll have you killed to keep the secret of his power. It will probably be his first command to me."

The Sheikh slowed down and considered. It did seem likely, now that he thought about it, that the Governor could prove dangerous. He wouldn't want rumours of his magic bottle getting back to his masters, the Council of Seventeen.

The Sheikh sighed. He'd been promised a lot of money by the Governor, but gold was of no use if you weren't alive to spend it.

"On the whole I think I'd better chuck you into the sea," he said to Asmodeus. "At least if I get rid of you I might get some cash out of the Governor without giving him reason to murder me."

Asmodeus was laughing so hard at the thought of anyone hoping to get money out of the Governor that it took him a while to register just what the Sheikh had said about throwing him into the sea.

"Oi! Wait a minute!" he squeaked. But the Sheikh could move fast when he was holding a bottled demon, and he was nearly at the beach.

"I mean, why not just let me out?" howled Asmodeus. "I'm no good to you if you're not giving me to the Governor, and nobody else is going to buy an unknown demon."

"You'd tear me to bits if I let you out," panted the Sheikh.

He drew back his arm to throw the bottle into the surging surf.

"Thanks a lot!" clamoured Asmodeus sarcastically, scrabbling at the glass. "I've just saved your life with that warning about the Governor!"

"I'm very grateful," the Sheikh assured him gravely, flinging the bottle as far out as he could.

The waves thundered over Asmodeus's bottle and he curled up and bounced like a rubber ball as it churned around in the surf.

Asmodeus had hoped to float, but the copper dragged the bottle down, deeper and deeper as it was sucked beyond the waves.

The pressure made Asmodeus's ears ring. Bumps and dongs and grating noises echoed through the bottle. It became darker and colder inside until Asmodeus shivered in inky blackness with his arms clasped round his knees.

Every so often a stray current or sandshark would jolt him against the cold glass.

Asmodeus started whistling to cheer himself up, but the sound dropped flat and dull inside the glass and he soon stopped.

Scrub-scrub-scrub rocked the bottle on the sand.

Asmodeus had no way of telling whether he had sat there for a day or a week or a year, but he was thoroughly bored by the time a net scooped him up.

He was lifted through levels of lightening green until the sunlight burst in through the thick glass of the bottle and made him cover his eyes. The harsh cries of the gulls echoed all around and made his ears ache.

"Yusuf! Yusuf! Look what I have found!" cried a fisherman, holding the bottle up to the sun.

Two tiny yellow eyes stared back at him. *Scritch-scritch-scritch* went Asmodeus's nails.

"It's a little red crayfish," said Yusuf, the other fisherman. "They like to hide in bottles and shiny things."

"No, it's not. It's Asmodeus," squeaked Asmodeus. "Let me out and I'll grant you a wish."

The fishermen were surprised, but they weren't stupid.

"It says here that you'll have to be my servant forever," said the young fisherman, reading the engraving on the bottle's copper rim.

"Look, I'll make it three wishes, all right? Now let me out," snarled Asmodeus.

"That's not what it says on the bottle," insisted the fisherman, and Asmodeus trembled. The laws of magic are unbending and if the fisherman insisted upon his rights, Asmodeus would be a slave for decades, even forever if the fisherman asked for eternal life.

"You could make me emperor of the world!" gloated the young fisherman.

"Get real!" hooted Asmodeus. "If I could make you emperor of the world, do you think I'd be stuck in this bottle?"

"He could give us riches beyond our wildest dreams!" said the older fisherman, peering in.

"Very well," said Asmodeus cunningly. "But I suggest you first agree on whose servant I'm going to be. The one who pulls the cork out is my boss, remember. The other one doesn't count."

"You will be mine," said the young fisherman, picking at the stopper. "I found you."

"But I am the elder," said Yusuf, snatching at the bottle. "I can command him more wisely for both our sakes."

The fishermen tugged at the bottle while Asmodeus egged them on. Pretty soon they began to fight in earnest and the boat rocked like a cockleshell.

With his bottle spinning on the planks, Asmodeus saw nothing except bare feet in a layer of silvery fish kicking this way and that, but he carried on shouting encouragement first to one and then the other in the hope that the boat would capsize. It was a Malay prehau with outriggers, though, and came nowhere near to tipping over.

In the end, the two fishermen ran out of strength and glared at each other across the bottle.

"You have a bloody nose," said Yusuf. "I'm sorry, brother."

"You won't be when you discover your black eye," said the young fisherman.

"This bottle has already brought us nothing but grief and violence," said Yusuf, rubbing his eye. "See how that little devil in it sits grinning at our fight? It will only get worse when he is your servant, or mine."

"Losing a brother is too high a price to pay for anything," agreed the young fisherman, and they picked up the bottle and dropped Asmodeus back overboard.

He didn't know whether to laugh at his escape from servitude or weep at being back in the depths.

Asmodeus screwed his face against the cold glass. He had landed in a kelp forest this time, so his view was a greenly limited one of rocks and kelp-moorings and slowly browsing perlemoen. There was no chance of a net scooping him out of this.

Groing-groing-groing grated the bottle on the rocks of the ocean bed.

A limpet blocked one of Asmodeus's windows. "Get off!" he roared, but it sucked on tightly and stared hideously at him for weeks.

An octopus tried to open the bottle and Asmodeus made himself appear as delicious as possible, but the octopus was a tiny one and its tentacles were too soft to unpick the seal.

It liked the bright bottle, though, and was still clutching the copper when it snagged a baited line with its other arms and was hoisted into the air.

"We've caught an octopus," said a new set of fishermen, Hollanders this time, who couldn't read the Arabic labelling.

"It's caught something too," they added.

"Yes, they like shiny things," said Asmodeus, in as fishermanly a voice as possible.

"That's right," agreed the fishermen, each thinking another had spoken.

"Let's use it to bait a lobster pot," suggested Asmodeus, "and see if it works on crayfish."

"Good idea," agreed the fishermen, and Asmodeus's bottle was sent back down into the green sea, this time inside a wicker lobster pot, together with a load of fish heads.

There were a lot of crayfish around in those days and it wasn't long before one of them came stalking into the basket.

It seized the bottle and tore at its copper binding.

"No! No, you fool!" yelled Asmodeus, capering madly. "This end! This end! Get the stopper out!"

He crammed himself into the neck of the bottle and scritched furiously with his nails.

The crayfish transferred its attention to the copper around the stopper and Asmodeus braced his legs and pushed with all his might.

A big crayfish can bend a coin in its jaws and crack open mussels with its pincers. Asmodeus was beside himself with excitement as the copper started to peel off.

But the basket was already jerking upwards. Asmodeus heaved and grunted as the water grew lighter and he and the crayfish rose towards the swaying leaves of kelp.

"GREEEEEAARGH!!!" he roared with effort, steam jetting from his ears. The stopper whanged out of the bottle like a bullet from a gun and Asmodeus shot through the opening and up into the sky, full-sized at last, in a cloud of steam and shattered basket slats.

The fishermen sat quietly as the bits of wicker and broken glass pattered down around them. Their eyes followed Asmodeus, arrowing home to Devil's Peak.

"You know," remarked the shaggiest one, mopping a cut which the exploding bottle had made on his cheek, "I'm glad we didn't open that bottle. I think that was Asmodeus."

"I wondered what had become of him," said the one with a wicker hoop around his neck.

"Did you notice that he was holding our crayfish?" asked the helmsman through the ruins of his hat.

"Thieving devil," they agreed, baiting another basket.

Nothing much had gone wrong in the Cape Hell, Asmodeus was relieved to discover.

He cleared a bit of sediment out of the geyser and then went looking for the Sheikh, but the Sheikh was a sensible man and had long since shipped out on a felucca bound for Zanzibar.

So the only real result of Asmodeus's experience was his new habit of muttering to himself and the big crayfish that lived in a tank beside his desk.

Nobody could understand why he kept dropping bits of fish into the tank, muttering "Your slightest wish is to me as the sternest of commands, O Master," but they supposed that he had his reasons.

Sakunaka, the Handsome Young Man

*A Shona tale from Zimbabwe, originally told
to* HUGH TRACEY *in the Karanga tongue. The
illustration is by* PADRAIC O'MEARA.

ONCE UPON A TIME, there was a widow who had a handsome son. His name was Sakunaka Mugwai. She did not want him ever to get married, because he would go away with his wife and leave her all alone. So, when he grew up, she made him promise that he would not marry any girl who ate food that she had cooked. The widow was a very good cook and everyone liked to eat her food.

It was not long before the fame of this young man spread all through the countryside and young girls would come from near and far to try to see for themselves the beauty of Sakunaka. When they arrived at his home, his mother would greet the girls and say, "Girls, you have come a long way, you must be hungry. I will give you some porridge to eat."

"Thank you, Mother," they would reply, and when she had cooked the food they would eat it, there under the trees, outside the village.

Then the mother of Sakunaka would go to the hut of her son, stand outside the door and sing:

> Sakunaka, my son!
>> Some girls have come to see you.
> *Mother, what have you cooked?*
>> Porridge, my son, Mugwai.
> *Did they eat any?*
>> Yes, yes, my son.
> *Then send them all away.*

So the mother of Sakunaka would send the girls away.

Several groups of girls came to the village to see the handsome young man, and each time the mother of Sakunaka would offer them food to eat and they would accept. Each time she would sing her song and each time Sakunaka would tell her to send the girls away.

Now, one group of ten girls had noticed that anyone

who ate the food which his mother had cooked was sent away and could not see Sakunaka. So they made a plan. They would take their own food with them, hide it in the bushes near the village, and eat it together in secret.

When they came near the village, the mother of Sakunaka greeted them and said, "Girls, you have come a long way and must be hungry. I will give you some porridge."

"No, Mother, thank you. We are not hungry," said the girls.

"O-ho!" said the mother. "Then you must be tired and want to sleep." She showed them to a hut where they could spend the night, for she was sure they would be hungry by morning. But during the night the girls got up, left the hut and went out into the bush where they had hidden their supply of food. They ate their meal and returned to the hut.

Early in the morning the mother of Sakunaka went to their hut and said, "Now, girls, you must be hungry indeed. Here is some porridge I have brought you."

"No, Mother, thank you," said the girls. "We are not hungry."

"Oh, dear me," said the mother. "What shall I do? They do not want to eat my food!"

She kept the girls sitting in the shade outside the village for another day, and they slept once more in the same hut. During the night they went out to eat their food as before and returned again to the hut.

Early in the morning the mother of Sakunaka came again to their hut and said, "Now you really must be hungry, you girls. I have brought you your porridge."

"No, thank you, Mother. We are not hungry."

"Yo-we, yo-we!" said the mother of Sakunaka. "Now what shall I do?"

She went to the hut of her son and sang once more:

> Sakunaka, my son!
> Some girls have come to see you.
> *Mother, what have you cooked?*
> Porridge, my son, Mugwai.
> *Did they eat any?*
> No, no, my son!
> *Then bid them come inside.*

"Oh, my son," she cried, "now my days are finished. I must go now and die!"

"Go thou, Mother," he replied, "if this be your choice."

So the mother of Sakunaka put all her things together in one basket and went to a hut far away in the bush and there she died.

Then Sakunaka called the girls to his village and he chose the eldest of them to marry him.

The Mother Who Turned to Dust

This new creation myth from Malawi, written by children's book author and storyteller Kasiya Makaka Phiri and illustrated by Jonathan Comerford, reminds us how precious Mother Earth is. The mother figure in this story poses an interesting contrast with the one in the previous story.

ONCE UPON A TIME, the sun had a daughter. Like her father, she was a star of great brilliance, and she lived in the greater brilliance of the sun. She wore shoes made of shimmering star-shells and on her fingers, around her ankles, wrists and neck she wore sparklers collected from shooting stars. She shone brilliantly and lit up the void beyond the sun known as the sky. She reigned over it and ruled it with great wisdom, love and compassion.

One day, as she went about her rounds inspecting the uncountable planets of the vast universe, she saw a planet in a far-away corner. It was way out, almost at the very fingertips of the sun's reach. Its colours were all the shades of green and blue. She looked again and then she spoke.

"There on that planet," said the star to the sun, "that is where I want my throne. I want to spend my life in the richness of the green and the coolness of the blue."

The sun sighed. He looked at the star's great brilliance and sighed again. His eyes could see many years into the future.

"Everything is yours," he said. "You may go wherever you like. You may do whatever you want. Know this, though: you will have to shed most of your powers and leave them here. Your brilliant coat of pure light, your shoes of star-shells, your anklets and bracelets and necklaces with the twinkling of evening and morning stars – you cannot take them with you. The sensitive green on the planet could never take the heat of your brilliance, and the blue would dry up completely. However, instead of your brilliant attire, you may have three wishes which will be granted unconditionally."

"Very well," she said. "Let me think about it."

She thought and thought for years and years. For that is the way with the stars and the sun in the vast universe. Everything takes years and years to happen, although to them it really is only like a twinkling. At last, when she had thought enough, her mind was made up.

She agreed to shed her coat, to leave her cloak of dawn, her shoes of star-shells, her sandals of twilight and her slippers of the afterglow of dusk. In a dazzling brilliance she handed them to the sun. Then she said, "Now I'll go to the green and blue planet and be its mother."

"Take everything you need. Know that you will be greatly missed here even though you will be in our sight daily. Know also that you will always be welcome here," said the sun. "Alas, our glare may not always be pleasant to you on that little planet in your new body."

So, all around the sun, the rings, anklets, bracelets and necklaces of the star were strewn in a trail of stars, star-shells, twinkle-dust and sparkles spreading across the sky like a trail of spilled milk. They were arranged so she could see them from the green and blue planet. Thus she would remember where she had come from.

Finally she left, riding first on a shooting star which streaked across time and space. Later she rode on a single ray of light in the softness of a dawning day but she still had a long way to go. With her she had taken a hoe, a mortar and pestle, a winnowing basket, a water pot, a cooking pot, plates made of bamboo and wood, a little axe, a mat, and a great covering cloth. At last she rode on the first beam of light which was to reach the green and blue planet.

Landing on the planet, she saw how it was that it had looked so green from far off in the sky. The forests and grasslands were so beautiful it made her heart swell and grow even more gentle than it had been before. She looked lovingly at all the plants and they grew happily in her sight, the green becoming more lush. There were shrubs here, trees there, and over yonder there were blossoms in the many colours of the light that had come with her from her home so far away: yellow, orange, blue, purple, white, pink, lemon, lime, azure, aquamarine and countless in-between shades and hues.

"Children, I wish to have children. Many, many children," she said. "I want children to love. Children to run in the grass. Children to sing, children to laugh and voices to echo on the mountainsides. Children to call and cuddle, and when I grow old and helpless, children to look after me. Children to be my strength when I grow weak and faint from living. And when the time comes, children to lay me to sleep."

Her wish was granted and there were children. Oh, there were children! All around her. On one side, on the other. In front and behind. There were sons tall, lithe and so strong they could stand on one leg for hours. And there were sons gentle and kind who shared warmth and compassion even with those who couldn't run very fast or stand for as long. There were daughters, tall and strong like their brothers, who could run and leap like grassland gazelles all day long and not tire even a little. And there were daughters tender and lovely like flowers, loving like mothers, kind like brothers and compassionate like fathers.

They rallied around the daughter of the sun and called her Mother.

And so the star, daughter of the sun, who had reigned in the sky with immeasurable brilliance, became the Mother of All Children born on the green and blue planet.

She loved them all and cared for each one. The tall and the short children, the fat children and the lean, the dark, the pale and the golden. She cared for them all, both day and night.

There were children who walked and never ran, and children who ran and never walked. There were *mine* children who wanted everything for themselves. *Nothing* children who never said more than just one word: *nothing*. There were *I'll be back* children who came and left in a flash. *Not me* children who never admitted they had done anything wrong. *I don't know* children, *he started it* children, *she asked for it* children who were mean and inconsiderate, and many, many more children.

She cared for them and brought them rain and plenty. Knowing the ways of the sky, she also brought them sun and shine. And when it was time for the plants to rest, she brought in Autumn and Winter to put the plants to sleep.

She cared for the children while they were awake and while they slept. She was up earlier than anyone. With a big broom she would sweep and clean, and she would start early with her hoe to grow the food the children needed. For though they were voracious, she always had enough food for them to eat after all the running, the singing, the hiding and the seeking, and all the things children love to do all day long.

The Mother of All Children was very strong, but the years weighed heavily on her shoulders. And the children of the earth were changed. Once she complained to the sun, "They are all so changed. I have become nothing to them. I doubt if they even see me at all." The sun replied, "Remember, they are your children. They did not ask to be brought into the world. Work with them. You will find treasure where you least expect it, when you least expect it."

And so she worked, serving her children, who had begun to fight over things. They did not help each other or do anything for themselves, but were always crying and demanding her presence and attention.

"Oh, I'm hungry – oh, I'm thirsty – oh, I want this, I want that – carry me, cuddle me. You are the Mother, you brought us into this world. Take care of us."

And the Mother of All Children healed the hurts and fed hungry mouths and watered thirsty throats and nursed them into men and women. They wandered off to far-away places, coming back only once in a while and sometimes never at all. By now they had become so mean and wild they even killed each other.

Sadness started gnawing at the Mother's heart. Where she had once been tall and proud, she was now bent over with the pain and the shame that her children heaped on her as they blamed her for everything. They had not a single kind word for her, and sadness ate chunks out of her already bleeding heart.

And so it was that in the wind that howled and tore trees down, she sang to comfort herself as she worked. She sang in the cool breeze that kissed the day at dawn, as it gently shook the sleeping birds awake to sing the morning chorus. She sang in the drumming of the rain that poured down violently and snatched uncovered land, carrying it away to the sea. She sang in the silent drizzle that fell like feathers on top of the great mountains of the world. And in those places cold enough, she sang in the rain that turned into snow and in the rain that came down in lumps of angry hail.

Singing, she would scan the sky even in broad daylight, as if there were something there that would help her. Then, looking down at her work, she would sing some more. Sometimes when she was out collecting firewood in the forest or on the wooded plains, she would sing of forests, some of which had been torn to bits by her wandering children, who cut the trees and took away whole trunks that had taken years to grow, leaving the earth half destroyed and dying.

The Mother of All Children knew that her children did not care for the earth. They dug pits searching for precious metals and left the gaping wounds to bleed. As she wandered the earth, this was the song she sang. She sang it in small fragments, sometimes aloud, sometimes quietly:

> *You till me and turn me*
> *to harvest your heart's desire,*
> *till you leave me naked, wounded.*
> *Punishing droughts render me barren,*
> *torrential rains tear my flesh*
> *so all who pass by scoff and spit on me.*
> *And I endure everything.*
> *I, the Mother born to give,*
> *hold nothing back for myself.*
> *I feed the world and my children look on*
> *as I lie poisoned by their hand.*

Because the children's ears were not attuned to the music of the earth, they did not pay attention to what she sang. Only sometimes, when she sang at dusk, only sometimes, a heaviness descended on the hearts of the once gentle and compassionate children.

As the children scattered further afield still, each wanted to own more and more space. They got up every day and fought over trees. They fought over glittering rocks. They staked out bits of land.

"This tree is mine," here. "No, it's mine," there. "Mine, mine," everywhere.

They collected the birds from the forests and put them in cages with no room to fly. They scooped the fishes from the waters and put them in containers with no room to swim. They shot the animals just for fun and collected their heads and hides. Sometimes they trapped and gathered animals from the wilderness and shut them up in prisons. They cut the trees in the forests and laid them bare.

And so, when the earth grew tired and the Mother of All Children grew old and sickly and died, the children did not even know to care.

Upon her death she was granted her second wish: that her remains be clothed in black and she be allowed to continue serving her children as best she could. And so even in death she worked, every day and every night, wearing a black robe and black cape. She worked even harder now that she did not need to sleep. The children still did not care. They kept on calling, "Give me, give me, give me," and she continued serving without stopping.

Because she was now only a spectre, she never said anything. Her songs came in the night and at break of day only, because the wind found them in the valleys and the hills where their echoes still lingered.

The Mother took especial care of a child who had been born early in her time but who could not talk. The child had the most beautiful eyes and her dark hair, braided and beaded behind her, was strong. Just as her hair grew, her heart also grew. And as her heart grew, so did her legs and arms grow strong. She grew into a lovely young woman.

One day, as she was going about her chores, she suddenly stopped and looked up at the Mother. Then she spoke for the first time.

"Let me help you, Mother. Please sit down and rest." Her voice was kind and after she had spoken, a deafening silence fell. Kindness had long since left the planet and now everything seemed to stop, though only for a moment.

The Mother heaved a sigh. "Oh, thank you, my child," she said.

Through this one act of kindness the Mother was released. She fell to the ground in a heap and turned to dust. Her work was done. A great wind came and gathered her dust and blew it into the sky to form the Moon we see today. So her third wish, that a soft light might shine on her so that she might see her children and the green and blue planet every month of the year, was granted.

And to this very day, every month the Moon watches over her children fighting and quarrelling. She sees her daughters, led by the young woman, mending and healing, serving and saving, as she had done before them.

But the children of the daughters of the Moon still fight, still quarrel, still complain. And the Moon, seeing this, has to hide her face and weep before she can bear to take another look, showing first only a crescent of her face. Then she turns it more and more till her full face beams with love.

On such a night some catch the love and pass it round. Then the daughters of the Moon sing the song of those given to serve, wishing for one more wish: that the children may learn to love their Mother once more.

Mpipidi and the Motlopi Tree

A Tswana tale, retold by early childhood specialist
JOHANNA MORULE, about the heart's desire of a little boy.
The illustration is by JUDY WOODBORNE.

ONCE THERE WAS A BOY called Mpipidi. He lived in a small village, far out in the country where the motlopi trees grow and jackals howl at night. Mpipidi lived with his parents and his younger brother. Often he had wished for a sister. But this, his fondest wish, had not come true.

Mpipidi herded his father's cattle. Every morning before the sun rose he would take his provisions and drive the herd deep into the bush. Here he would climb into the highest motlopi tree and watch the cattle. He loved sitting up there, from where he could see the blue mountains in the distance, and where he was so high up that the eagle was his brother and the cloud was his sister. His sister? The thought made him sad.

When one of the cows strayed, Mpipidi would whistle softly. He whistled a sweet, haunting tune, like that of the honeybird calling a badger to a honeycomb. Then Mpipidi would chant:

Tswerr, tswerr!
My brown ones,
Do not stray
Tswerr, tswerr!
Or you'll be swallowed
By kgokgomodumo!
Tswerr, tswerr!

Then the stray cow would lift her head and return, grazing, towards Mpipidi in the motlopi tree. This magic saved Mpipidi the trouble of climbing up and down the tree to look for the cattle.

One day, Mpipidi took the cattle even further into the bush, and while he was looking for the tallest motlopi tree, he heard faint crying: "Nngee! Nngee!"

Mpipidi stopped and listened. Yes, there it was again: "Nngee! Nngee!"

He crawled under the dense branches of the motlopi

tree and there, in a newly woven basket, padded with soft skins of wild animals, he found a baby. Mpipidi carefully picked up the baby. It was a little girl. His heart beat faster . . . No, he could not take her home! Perhaps they would not believe his story or give her away. So he put the baby back into the basket and looked for another motlopi tree far away where he could hide her.

Then he took milk from his provisions and fed her. Soon the baby was happy and fell asleep. Mpipidi chopped some branches from thorn trees and laid them around her sleeping-place as a fence to protect her from wild animals.

That evening he told nobody about the baby. She remained his secret.

Every morning, from that day onwards, Mpipidi would take some goat's milk for the baby and some food for himself. Every morning he would drive the cattle deep into the bush. He would carefully approach the motlopi tree, and when he was near, he would softly sing:

A ga anke a lela –
Tshetsanyane – tshetsa!
Ngwanaa 'tlhare sa motlopi –
Tshetsanyane – tshetsa!
Motlopi le Mpipidi –
Tshetsanyane – tshetsa!
Ako a l'le a ree: Nngee!
Tshetsanyane – tshetsa!

A little voice would answer, "Nngee! Nngee!" and Mpipidi would know that the baby was still alive. He would remove one of the fencing branches, pick her up and feed her, singing all the while. When the baby was well fed, he would carefully put her back into the basket under the motlopi tree and cover her with the skins. Then he would replace the fencing branch.

This continued until his mother guessed that Mpipidi had a secret. So she said to her husband, "What do you think about this boy? Why does he insist on following the cattle every day, even if the weather is bad?"

The father added, "And why doesn't he want his brother to go with him? How will his brother ever learn to look after the cattle? I will follow him tomorrow morning!"

The next morning, the father followed Mpipidi. He stayed far enough behind him not to be seen, but near enough to hear his son's whistling and singing.

Mpipidi drove the cattle into the grazing place, whistling all the way.

Deep in the bush, the whistling stopped. The father walked a little faster and saw how Mpipidi carefully approached the tall motlopi tree. When he was near the tree, the father heard him sing softly:

A ga anke a lela –
Tshetsanyane – tshetsa!
Ngwanaa 'tlhare sa motlopi –
Tshetsanyane – tshetsa!
Motlopi le Mpipidi –
Tshetsanyane – tshetsa!
Ako a l'le a ree: Nngee!
Tshetsanyane – tshetsa!

Then the father heard the little voice: "Nngee! Nngee!" His eyes widened. Wasn't that a baby's cry?

He saw Mpipidi remove one of the fencing branches, pick up a baby and feed it. When the baby was well fed, Mpipidi carefully put her back into the basket under the tree and covered her with the skins. Then he replaced the fencing branch.

So this was his son's secret! The father immediately returned home and told his wife what he had seen.

The next morning, while it was still dark, Mpipidi's father took his wife to the motlopi tree. Long before anyone else in the village was awake, they were back with the baby.

As usual, Mpipidi took his provisions and the goat's milk and drove the cattle deep into the bush. Carefully he approached the tall motlopi tree. When he was near the tree, he softly sang his song. He listened, but there was no little voice. He repeated the tune. Still no answer. His voice trembled as he sang again and again. Only dead silence came from the motlopi tree.

So Mpipidi pulled away the branches – but the baby was gone! He lay down under the motlopi tree and cried bitterly. In the afternoon he drove the cattle back home.

When he got home, he went into the hut and sat down so that the smoke from the open fire stung his eyes. Tears rolled down his cheeks and his heart was heavy with fear and sorrow.

"Why are you crying, Mpipidi?" his mother asked. He told her his eyes were smarting from the smoke. But when she asked him to go out into the fresh air, Mpipidi only shook his head.

"Mpipidi," said his mother, "we know that you are crying for the baby you have hidden under the motlopi tree."

Mpipidi was shocked, and he stopped crying.

"Come with me," his mother said. And she called his father too. Carefully she approached the sleeping-hut. At the door she softly sang:

> A ga anke a lela –
> *Tshetsanyane – tshetsa!*
> Ngwanaa 'tlhare sa motlopi –
> *Tshetsanyane – tshetsa!*
> Motlopi le Mpipidi –
> *Tshetsanyane – tshetsa!*
> Ako a l'le a ree: Nngee!
> *Tshetsanyane – tshetsa!*

Then they heard the little voice: "Nngee! Nngee!"

Mpipidi looked at his mother. Then he looked at his father. "Yes, Mpipidi," said his father, "we know that was your secret! Was that why you did not want your brother to herd the cattle with you?"

Mpipidi did not answer. He took the bottle and sat down to feed the baby as usual.

His mother gazed at him and saw how much he loved the baby.

"Give me Keneilwe – your baby sister," she said. Mpipidi gave her the baby. He was filled with deep joy to see his sister in his mother's arms.

Keneilwe grew up to be a beautiful girl and a loving sister. Her name reminded everyone of her unusual beginnings: Keneilwe, "The one who is given".

A ga a-nke a le-la / Tshet-sa-nya-ne, tshet-sa! Ngwa-naa 'tlha-re sa mo-tlo-pi / Tshet-sa- nya-ne, tshet-sa! Mo-tlo-pi le Mpi-pi-di / Tshet-sa-nya-ne, tshet-sa! A-ko a l'le a ree: Ngee, Ngee! Tshet-sa-nya-ne, tshet-sa!

Fesito Goes to Market

A market story set in Uganda, by children's book author and novelist
CICELY VAN STRATEN. *The theme is universal: a triple reward*
for three good deeds. The illustrator is DIEK GROBLER.

ONE MORNING FESITO WOKE early, at the matulutu-lu, the first cock-crow, before the sun was up. This day he would go to market on his father's bicycle, for his father lay ill with fever. This day he would ride like a man with the bananas; he would ride with his head held high, a man among men.

He rolled up his mat and looked out. The sky was pale yellow behind the banana trees where the sun would rise, and dew lay on the grass. It was a fine morning to be going to market all on his own, to bring back money in his pockets and count it out in front of everyone, in the evening, as his father usually did. "Eh-eh," they would say as the cents and shillings clattered from his hands into the wooden bowl, "so much money! Truly, Fesito, you are clever. You are a man who knows the world!"

Outside in the cool dawn his mama was tying up the bananas. "Fesito, come and eat!" she said.

"Eh, Mama. Wasusiotiano! How are things with you today?"

"Bulungi! Good, my child." She strapped the bananas onto the rack of the bicycle that leant against a tree. Then she went for the milk gourd and gave Fesito a bowl of porridge. Beneath the mvule tree he sat and ate his porridge while his mama put small change into a handkerchief and twisted it round many times.

Fesito took the money and put it deep in his pocket. He could feel it, heavy against his leg. It was safe there. Then he pushed the bicycle out of the yard and onto the road.

"Weraba, Fesito!" cried his mama. "Goodbye!"

"Weraba, Mama!" he called and began to run with the bicycle. But it was so heavy! Heavier than when he played with it in the evenings after his father had come home from the market. The big load of bananas pulled it from side to side. First it leant this way, then that way, and the bicycle skidded and slid over the red ground. Aaaiee! Fesito clucked his tongue and he struggled to hold the handlebars steady. "Surely, my father is very strong indeed, to ride so easily to market every day! But today I shall be like my father too. No one shall say that I, Fesito, stumble under the load."

He pushed and pushed the bicycle till he came to where the road ran downhill. Then he hopped on and leant forward and rode away. The cool air streamed across his face and the hornbills flew out of his way.

"*Knaaaaak! Knaaaaaaaaak!*" they honked.

"Yes! Make way for one who is greater than thou!" he called to them. "Make way for me, Fesito, who rides as a man among men to market!"

The sun came up behind him and shone on the banana leaves. The red hibiscus flowers began to unfold and the scent of frangipani was sweet upon the breeze. The bulbuls sang in the cassias.

The sun rose higher and the mist in the valleys floated away. Soon, on the road ahead, Fesito saw an old man. He was walking, bent over, with a basket in his hand. It was old Musoke.

"Wasusotio, Old One!" cried Fesito as he rode up.

"Wasusotio, Fesito," said old Musoke. "What is the matter with your father today, that he lends you his bicycle to go wobbling on to market?"

Fesito was cross with Musoke. Did the old never learn manners?

"My father has the fever, Old One. *I'm* taking the bananas to market today."

Old Musoke groaned and rubbed his back. His little black eyes amidst their many wrinkles looked up at Fesito. "My child, I am old and my back is stiff – aieeee! – it is very stiff. Won't you take my pawpaws to the market and save me the walking?"

There were many pawpaws and Musoke's basket looked very heavy. Fesito would have to tie it to the handlebars – and think how difficult it would be to ride! Still, it would not be good manners to refuse an old man.

"All right," he said, "I'll take the pawpaws."

"There's a good child," said old Musoke. "I'll tell your father he has a well-mannered son."

But Fesito sighed as he took the pawpaws. He knew that old Musoke would have forgotten his kindness by that very afternoon and that the next time he saw him he would be as cross as ever.

He tied the pawpaws to the bicycle and turned to the old man. Musoke had already sat down and was taking out his tobacco pouch.

"Weraba, Old One," said Fesito.

"Weraba, Fesito," said old Musoke as he lay back in the shade of a cassia tree and filled his clay pipe.

Now the bike was even heavier, and Fesito's legs ached as he pedalled. He was disappointed. He had thought it would be very grand to go to market on his father's bicycle, but somehow it was very difficult. "Still," he thought, "I am a man among men today. That is something."

The sun rose higher and soon there were many people on the road going to market.

"Wasusotio, Nalubale!" he called. Nalubale waved. She was very pretty. What a pity she was an older girl, and married. He liked Nalubale very much.

"Wasusotio!" she called. "Ride well!"

All along the sides of the road were women carrying water pots and children running behind them with hoops and sticks or small baskets of peanuts.

"Fesito, child! Wait a minute!"

He stopped. Who had called this time? Then he saw Kasiingi running up with three chickens hanging in a bunch, bound by the feet.

"Here, child, take my chickens to the market for me,

please. It will save me much work. Be sure to bring me the right change – five shillings each. No, make the big one seven shillings."

She held out the chickens.

"Do they think I'm a mule, to carry all their things?" thought Fesito. "Would they do this to my father?"

"Kasiingi," he said, "where shall I carry three chickens with all these bananas and pawpaws?"

Kasiingi looked at the bundles. She screwed up her eyes and pointed to the top of the bananas. "There, child! There! Are you blind? There's room for ten chickens on top of your bananas!"

She took some banana-leaf twine and tied the three chickens on top of the bananas. Now the pile on the bike was so high Fesito could hardly reach the top with his hands.

"Mind you ride carefully! If my chickens arrive at the market dead, I shall tell your father!"

And he knew that Kasiingi never forgot to tell his father such things. He sighed and got onto the bicycle again.

"Weraba, Fesito! Don't forget my money!"

"Weraba, Kasiingi."

Now it was very hot. The sweat ran down his face and down his back under his shirt. His breath came in gasps. Would he get to market on time? It was further than he'd thought. Every now and then he rode over a bump and the chickens clucked "*taaaaaak!*" very crossly.

Presently he saw a small boy walking ahead of him. He was very thin and he walked slowly and not in a straight line. It was Kikyo. Kikyo had been very ill. Where was he going today?

"Eh, Kikyo!" he cried, riding up. "Look at me! I'm taking the bananas to market. My father has the fever. Where are you going, Kikyo?"

"To the hospital, to get my medicine," said Kikyo.

"Won't you let me ride with you, Fesito, please? My legs are tired already."

"And where would you sit?" cried Fesito. All his crossness boiled up inside him. "It is hard work for me with all these things. Old Musoke made me carry his pawpaws and Kasiingi made me carry her chickens. There is no room for mere children, Kikyo. Am I a pack mule, to carry everyone to market? Use your own legs! Weraba!" He rode on quickly, leaving Kikyo behind.

But somehow Kikyo's face was still in front of him. Kikyo's eyes were big and his face was very sharp and thin. His ribs stuck out above his stomach and the joints of his legs were swollen, his arms and legs very thin. Should he not, after all, have taken Kikyo to the hospital? Kikyo had asked nicely. Kasiingi and old Musoke had not.

He sighed and stopped. He turned round and called, "Kikyo! Come here quickly! Hurry! I'll take you to town if you sit very still and do not fall off. Hurry!"

Kikyo came shuffling up. "Webali, Fesito. Thank you, my big friend."

"Climb up and sit on the saddle," said Fesito. "And sit very still. If you wobble, the bicycle will topple over and everything will fall off."

"Eh," said Kikyo and climbed onto the saddle. He looked very pleased. "Webali, my friend," he said again. "I shall sit as still as a mouse."

Fesito pushed and pushed. Only on the downhill could he ride. His legs and arms and back ached. It was as if the bicycle did not want to move at all. The road wavered like water in the heat and the screaming of the cicadas made his head swim. At last there was only one more hill to go.

Then Kikyo said, "I'm hungry, Fesito. Can I take a banana?"

"No, they're to be sold at the market!" said Fesito.

"What will my father say if they're eaten on the way by children?"

"Eh," said Kikyo. "I see."

But then Fesito thought of how thin Kikyo was. How small and hungry-looking. And he was only seven. He had suffered a lot for such a young one.

"Kikyo," he said severely, "you may take one banana. Only one! Take it very carefully and do not upset the pile."

"Webali," said Kikyo. He took a banana, peeled it and began to eat. "It is very good, Fesito. Webali."

And now they stood at the top of the hill that overlooked the town, lying red and brown between the yellow cassia trees. There were many people at the market under the mango trees. The men in their long robes stood talking, and some were drinking beer. Women squatted by the stalls, their long bright dresses all the colours of the rainbow, like colourful birds resting in the shade.

"Eh, it is good to be going to market!" said Fesito. "It is good to be a man among men, Kikyo."

"Truly, Fesito, you are strong," said Kikyo and took another bite of banana.

And Fesito's heart swelled out, big and full inside him, and he stood very straight as he looked down on the marketplace.

Just then there was loud laughter behind them. Fesito turned and saw Bosa, Kagwe, Waswa and Matabi run out from the bushes. He did not like Bosa and Bosa did not like him. He turned away from them and began to push the bicycle downhill.

"Look who goes there! Look who goes wobbling on his father's bicycle that is much too big for him! Who goes there, loaded with rubbish!" shouted Bosa and ran alongside him. Kagwe, Waswa and Matabi jeered and shouted.

"Look who rides to market eating a banana like a baboon!" cried Matabi, pointing at Kikyo.

"You're jealous because you have no bicycles to ride!" shouted Fesito and rode on faster downhill.

"You lie, you lie!" shouted Bosa.

"We'll teach you to shout so rudely!" cried Kagwe.

Bosa ran ahead and broke a stick from a cassia tree. He held out the stick so that it would catch the spokes of the wheels and send the bicycle with Fesito and Kikyo crashing to the ground.

Fesito saw him and tried to steer aside but Bosa dodged in front again. There was nothing Fesito could do. He saw he would fall with the bike and Kikyo, and the bananas and pawpaws and chickens would be squashed.

"Ha, ha! You who think you are a man among men!" laughed Bosa. "You'll cry like a baby when you fall in the road!" Bosa came closer with his stick. Just at that moment a half-eaten banana hit him across the eyes. Then a banana peel, thrown very hard, flew *smack!* into his face. Kikyo laughed. Bosa staggered to the side of the road, wiping his face.

"Ride, Fesito, ride!" shouted Kikyo, laughing still.

But Matabi, who was bigger than them all, ran up from behind. "You! You baboon! You think you can be rude to us! Let me show you what I do to the boastful!" He reached up to pull down the pile of bananas. But suddenly he cried, "Ow! Ai!" and jumped back in surprise. The chickens had pecked crossly at his face and arms.

"Ah!" thought Fesito. "Now I'm glad I took the chickens for Kasiingi!"

But they had not reckoned with Waswa. He picked up a stone and threw it at Fesito. *Smack!* It hit him in the back and it hurt very much. Waswa ran beside them, jeering, "Little cowards! Little cowards who run away instead of turning to fight! Ba, little cowards!"

He bent to pick up another stone when *bonk*, a hard green pawpaw flew through the air and hit him on the ear. Waswa ran away into the bushes holding his head and howling.

"Ah," thought Fesito, "I'm glad I did not refuse old Musoke!"

And Kikyo chuckled behind him, "Ride faster, Fesito! No one can catch us now!"

Fesito pedalled faster and faster. *Zizzzzz!* sang the bicycle. Kikyo's laughter rang in his ears. Faster they went and faster. No one could catch them now! *Zizzzzzzzz!* ticked the wheels – *zizzzzzzzz!*

"Kikyo!" called Fesito. "You are a clever child, even if you are so small. Webali! Without the banana skin and the pawpaw so swiftly thrown, we would now be lying in the road while those thieves stole our things!"

"I'm glad I was kind to Kikyo!" he thought.

Now they sped down the road as if they were flying. Trees and houses flashed past. And then suddenly they burst into the marketplace. People and chickens and dogs scattered out of the way.

"Hey! Fesito! Is the evil one chasing you? Mind my peanuts! Mind my eggs! Mind my pawpaws!"

"Fesito! Mwana! Son of my brother!" called his aunt from her stall. "Is this how you come to market, like a whirlwind on the plain?" But his aunt was smiling and he, Fesito, with Kikyo on the seat behind him, rode into market with his head held high. He laughed and Kikyo echoed his laughter and his back was stiff with pride. He, Fesito, had brought the bananas of his father and the pawpaws of old Musoke and the chickens of Kasiingi to market without harm. He, Fesito, rode as a man among men!

Sannie Langtand and the Visitor

Another Cape tale by ALEX D'ANGELO, *about Sannie Langtand, the tough old witch from Kalk Bay, Boggom, her dogsbody-baboon, and their friend, Slangbek, the treasure-loving dragon with the fiery breath who can travel through time. In this story, narrated by Boggom, they travel to foreign parts. Illustrated by* JO HARVEY.

IT WAS A GREY DAY in the Cape. Rain was coming in clouds over the dark mountains and the sea was snapping irritably at the harbour wall. Mountain water kept seeping into Sannie Langtand's cave and making her firewood wet. After a while she threw down the bellows and stamped on them in rage. "Go and tell Slangbek to come and give me a light!" she commanded me. So out I had to go into the cold and the rain.

Maybe I should warn you that Sannie Langtand is the meanest, scrawniest witch in the Kalk Bay mountains, and Slangbek is a savage old dragon who spends most of his time draped over a pile of loot in his cave. That is, when he is not out flying or smoking with Sannie Langtand.

And then there is me, Boggom. I'm Sannie Langtand's familiar, which means that I do most of the dirty work around her cave and that she sometimes rides me on business when she can't persuade Slangbek to give her a lift. I'm a baboon, by the way, which is quite a nice thing to be if you live up on Kalk Bay Mountain, or even if you don't. It's easy to pick me out from the other roadside baboons since I wear long Persian slippers and sometimes carry a shovel for digging up the "Don't Feed the Baboons" signs put up by all those people who've never had to eat Sannie Langtand's cooking.

I was not at all sure that Slangbek would agree to come out in such weather, but when I found him in his cave he was bored and wanted someone to talk to. Also I think he felt in the mood for a bowl of Sannie Langtand's sour milk.

To my relief Slangbek decided to walk rather than fly. As he trundled through the bush, leaving a trail like a forestry path, he spread a wing for me to shelter under, like a large leathery umbrella. We walked up and down and round about so that Slangbek could snuffle around all the places that interested him. I didn't mind, since standing against a dragon in wet weather is as good as being beside a hot stove.

By the time we got home Sannie Langtand had been kept waiting a good long time and was ready to pick a fight with anything. She hardly seemed at all grateful when Slangbek stuck his head in and huffed her fire alight. She just started puffing on her black clay pipe without a word of thanks and was soon shrouded in smoke. Slangbek snatched up a mouthful of old coals and started smoking the way he likes to, and between the two of them the air in the cave was getting pretty dark and thick.

"Wet day to be out," said Slangbek, hoping for his milk.

"Foggy day to be out," snapped Sannie Langtand from the corner of her rat-trap mouth. "Got lost, did you? Had to ask directions on Main Road? And all the while here I was dying for a smoke and no fire to be had at all!"

"Now listen, you old heks!" said Slangbek, beginning to show a bit of fire at the corners of his mouth. "I never get lost, not in time nor in space nor in the places between the stars! I'm not taking that from an old hag who needs a baboon to find her way about!"

By now the atmosphere in the cave was getting hot with more than smoke, so I edged my way past Slangbek and out into the cold air.

The first thing I saw when my eyes had cleared, apart from Slangbek's long tail trailing away from the cave, was a very wet-looking foreign gentleman staring with some concern at Slangbek's backside. If he thinks that's ugly, I thought to myself, I can't wait till he sees Slangbek's face, let alone Sannie Langtand, who's worse than a dragon at both ends.

The foreign gentleman bowed low, until only his nose and slippers could be seen behind a huge turban. "Most esteemed Sir!" he cried as I scratched myself thoughtfully, wondering what to do with him. "I am an adventurer from the distant land of Persia, a messenger of emirs and sultans from the rolling desert sands. Alas, I find myself in a state of great distress, unable to make my way back home and report to the Pasha himself." The stranger held up the soggy ruins of a magic carpet, all mildewed and come to pieces in the Cape winter. "To pile sorrow upon sorrow, my preferred means of transport has chosen this moment to divest itself of its powers of flight, not to mention its ability to travel home through time."

"Eh?" said I, like a simple, hairy fellow from the hills, which is what I am, of course. The little gentleman straightened up and realised that he was talking to a baboon.

"I'm lost," he said. "I need directions and my time-travelling magic carpet has come to bits and won't fly any more."

"Now why couldn't you say that in the first place?" I said, thinking that anyone who stood babbling about directions within tail-pulling distance of a dragon needed his head examined. As a rule, the only sensible direction to take is away from the dragon. Of course I'd normally have chased him off with a few good barks and bites, since Sannie Langtand doesn't much care for visitors, but I was mindful of the hissings and shoutings coming from the cave and thought an interesting foreign gentleman would be a good distraction for them, even if he did land up going flappity, flappity down the mountain on little webbed feet. That's what happens to unwelcome visitors in these parts: Sannie Langtand makes frogs of them.

The foreign gentleman seemed quite reluctant to squeeze past Slangbek and into the cave, but I had a good grip on him. "Visitor!" I called out as we came into the glow of the firelight, in case Sannie Langtand was about to do anything embarrassing, like clonk Slangbek over the head with her iron pot.

Slangbek was quite pleased to see the visitor, but Sannie Langtand was still as bad-tempered as ever.

"Can't find your way back?" she hooted mockingly once he'd told his tale with much bowing and grovelling. "What kind of explorer do you call yourself? Just turn your back on where you've got to and follow your nose back home again. That's what I do! Even this old lizard Slangbek can manage it half the time." Sannie Langtand drummed her fingers on her nose as she said this, and I must say that it is quite true that Sannie Langtand's long snout is perfect for following since it sticks out like a compass needle and is covered with stiff hairs that twitch like antennae in the dark.

"A most enormous nose it is too, dear Madam," gibbered the foreign gentleman before he could stop himself. "Frog time," I thought to myself, and I would have been right except that Slangbek interrupted and saved him from a life of croaking on the lily pads.

"I am getting very fed up of this, Old Heks," he hissed, and the heat from his mouth was like a furnace door opening and slamming on each word. "I've known men like this in the days of pirate dhows. I could take him home with my eyes shut. Do you think you could do better by sniffing out the way with your great snonker?"

"Well, why don't you shut your eyes and we'll find out," snarled Sannie Langtand, reaching for the heavy pot. But Slangbek wasn't going to be fooled that easily. He kept his eyes open and Sannie Langtand's hand drifted innocently back to her side.

"If you're so sure you can guide him home, then I'll take you a bet on it," said Slangbek, licking his lips with a forked tongue. "That jar of sour milk against a bright copper pot from my hoard."

"Done!" snapped Sannie Langtand, who had always wanted one of Slangbek's pots. "You flap and I'll steer."

We all went outside to climb on Slangbek. The foreign gentleman had to be helped up quite roughly. "Really, most noble Sir and Madam, simple directions to the nearest magic-carpet repairman are all that is required," he wailed in a thin voice.

"Shut up," said Sannie Langtand, quite pleasantly for her. I said nothing at all. As far as I'm concerned, riding Slangbek is better than running up mountains with a witch on your back.

Slangbek flapped off the mountainside and swooped over the town. The houses looked like toys far below us. Soon we were deep in the grey cloud and flecks of frost glittered in my fur.

"Picture clearly where you want to go and hold the picture in your mind! I'll pick it up from there!" roared Slangbek. "Assuming that you have a mind, Old Heks," he added, not quite softly enough, so that Sannie Langtand thumped him hard on his knobbly head.

But Sannie Langtand had a bet to win, so she let Slangbek peer inside her mind. Judging by his shudders, he didn't much care for what she kept there. And when she'd made her picture good and sharp, Sannie Langtand leaned forward with her stringy hair whipping in the wind and howled directions in Slangbek's ear.

"Sand!" she shouted. "That's what I'm thinking of! Lots of sand. Like they have in Persia!"

"Well, if you're quite sure," he rumbled, and we disappeared, leaving a dragon-shaped gap in the cloud that slammed shut behind us like a thunderclap.

It never takes long to get anywhere when Slangbek does that particular trick. There's just a sudden lurch and you're where you want to be. Unless you do something silly, of course, like forgetting to keep your place in time.

"Aha!" chortled Sannie Langtand as we appeared beside a huge sand dune. "Right first time. Sand I aimed for and sand I got."

"I'm afraid not, Old Heks," said Slangbek. "It's more or less the right area but you're off course a bit timewise; a couple of million years or so, I should think."

"Says who?" snapped Sannie Langtand aggressively.

"Says him," answered Slangbek, nodding at a large Tyrannosaurus Rex that had just trundled round the dune and was standing grinning toothily at us. The foreign gentleman pulled his turban down over his eyes and began gnawing frantically on the tassel. I pushed my head past him and barked in Sannie Langtand's ear.

"Think of big turbans," I advised urgently, hoping we would hit more modern times.

"Run!" she shouted to Slangbek, who needs to be flying before he can play his disappearing trick. Slangbek scuttled up to the top of the dune. Behind us we could hear the *doof, doof, doof* of heavy dinosaur footsteps as Slangbek launched himself on spread wings.

He circled once over the dunes, looking down at the running dinosaur.

"I noticed that you didn't try clonking that one with a pot," he remarked to Sannie Langtand. The mistress was too busy getting her thoughts together to answer.

After a moment she leaned forward again and howled directions against the blast of the wind. I hoped she had the right picture in mind this time and wasn't thinking of anything unpleasant.

When we reappeared we were still flying and I was glad that Slangbek was playing it safe. We were high above a blue ocean, as far from sand as we could possibly be. There was a foreign smell to the air and the sun

was brassy and strong, but I didn't see any big turbans. Perhaps Sannie Langtand's concentration had slipped at the last minute and she had put us off course again.

"So where are the turbans?" I asked, but got no answer from Sannie Langtand or Slangbek.

"Excuse me," said the foreign gentleman uncertainly, "I seem to see another dragon or two over there."

I could feel Slangbek's sides grow warmer with interest as he dipped a wing and swooped across the sea. After a while we could see that they were not proper dragons like Slangbek but just brightly painted wooden boats with fiercely carved dragon faces and sails that were ribbed like Slangbek's wings.

"Chinese junks!" trumpeted Slangbek, not sounding as disappointed as I'd thought he'd be. "Dragon boats, they call them. I'll show you a thing or two now, Sannie Langtand."

He swooped up and down ostentatiously until we were seen. A great commotion burst out on the ships and swarms of men appeared from below. They knelt down and began knocking their heads on the deck.

"Big hats!" I cried out, because some of them were wearing huge, round hats like dustbin lids.

"Wrong sort," said Sannie Langtand sourly. "I was thinking of turbans. Mind must have wandered just a little, what with the other big lizard and all. Why are they banging their heads like that?"

Slangbek started laughing, a horrible sound, all *Snurff-Snurrf-Snurrf.* "They're kowtowing," he sniggered. "It's an act of worship. *Dragon* worship, Sannie Langtand, in case you were thinking it's for you. Now that's what I call respect. Could do with more of that where I come from, I can tell you."

"We kneel down to bow like that in Persia," chipped

in the foreign gentleman ingratiatingly. He squeaked as Sannie Langtand turned round slowly and he found himself looking into her beady eyes from a range of about two nose-lengths. "Not to dragons, of course," he gibbered. "No, no, no, ha, ha! No, no. Not to dragons. You see we shoot arrows at drag. . . er, hum." He stuffed the tassel of his turban back into his mouth and chomped at it energetically.

The thump of Slangbek's wingbeats faltered as he thought about that bit. He craned his neck back until he was staring at us upside down.

The folk on the boats loved that manoeuvre, but I wasn't quite so keen since it gave me a new angle on all the ugly parts that I'd more or less become used to.

"So you want me to take him back to where all the arrows are?" said Slangbek to Sannie Langtand.

"Don't be a sissy," said Sannie Langtand, who was determined to get her copper pot. "Anyway, just think of the good impression you'll make, coming back with this fellow. It might stop them shooting at dragons for good."

"I know a better way to stop them shooting at dragons," muttered Slangbek, turning round again. "This is your last try, Old Heks. After this the milk is mine. And so is our little arrow-shooter," he added as an afterthought. He made a last few swoops over the dragon boats while Sannie Langtand summoned her concentration.

"Think of proper turbans," I advised her.

Sannie Langtand shrilled her commands and we disappeared from the big blue sky above the boats like a burst of fireworks, Slangbek launching gouts of flame to keep the sailors religious.

"Bull's-eye," gloated Sannie Langtand as we burst into existence over a city of tall towers, all ending in points like onions. It was surrounded by sand and there

were lots of palm trees and men in turbans like the foreign gentleman's. The best clue was a huge sign on the dunes near a landing strip for flying carpets. "Welcome to Persia", it said.

Something went *fwip* as it shot past us, and a nasty sharp sound it was too. I looked up to see a stripy arrow arcing up against the sun. Lots more men with bows were running out on rooftops and taking aim at us.

"Land so I can deliver him!" howled Sannie Langtand, her mind full of copper pots.

"Land and deliver him yourself!" grunted Slangbek, hammering upwards as fast as he could flap. A whole stream of *fwips* were coming past us now and Slangbek was swerving like a swallow to avoid them.

"I want him home on the ground!" screamed Sannie Langtand, who knew that Slangbek could be counted on to weasel out of the bet if given any excuse at all.

"I don't have to land for that," said Slangbek. "*Hou vas!*" he shouted, which means "hold tight" in Afrikaans. Now Sannie Langtand and I understood him very well and clung on tightly, but while Afrikaans has a few Arabic words in it, "Hou" and "vas" aren't two of them, and when Slangbek rolled over on his back the foreign gentleman disappeared with a whoosh.

"Nooooo!" screamed the foreign gentleman, seeing the town spiralling up at him.

"Nooooo!" screamed Sannie Langtand, seeing her copper pot disappearing like mist.

Quick as a flash we snatched for him. I got the heels and Sannie Langtand got the turban and for a minute he swung between us like a hammock. Then his feet shot free of his slippers and he was unwinding downwards as his turban uncoiled, with Sannie Langtand holding cursing on to one end and the foreign gentleman going down like a yo-yo on the other.

The last I saw of him he had his arms wrapped round

teacher, then as head of a primary school in the Rustenburg area and eventually as an educational planner for the Bophuthatswana department of education. She wrote several school readers and served on the Setswana Language Board.

During the turn of the previous century **Julius Oelke** worked as missionary of the Berlin Mission Church in what was then Tanganyika and is now Tanzania. He did important literary conservation work by writing down in German the African stories he heard in Kibena, thereby ensuring that these little-known stories from the oral tradition are today available in written form.

Kasiya Makaka Phiri was born in 1948 in what was then Southern Rhodesia and is now Zimbabwe and grew up in Malawi. His interest in writing started at the age of thirteen, and he had his first success in 1969 as author of a radio drama. His poetry has been published in magazines in Malawi, Canada, the USA, India, South Africa, Nigeria and the UK. Since 1983 he has been living in the USA as a political exile.

Diana Pitcher was born in Natal in 1921 and obtained a degree in English from the University of Natal. She became a schoolteacher and worked in Natal, Zimbabwe, England and Europe. She is best known for two collections of African folklore entitled *The Calabash Child* and *The Mischief Maker*, both of which were published in eight African languages.

Marguerite Poland grew up on a smallholding just outside Port Elizabeth in the Eastern Cape. She studied Xhosa and Anthropology at Rhodes University and then obtained an Honours degree in Xhosa from Stellenbosch University, an MA in Zulu Folklore from the University of Natal and finally a doctorate in Zulu Literature from the same university. She has published numerous children's books and three adult novels to great critical acclaim and has twice received the prestigious Percy Fitzpatrick Award for Children's Literature. She lives in KwaZulu-Natal.

Minnie Postma grew up on a Free State farm near the Lesotho border. As child she could speak Sesotho just as well as Afrikaans and avidly listened to the stories told round the dung fires in the evenings. She made such a thorough study of this particular story-telling tradition that she was later able to create her own tsomo (stories) in the Sotho idiom.

Linda Rode is well known as compilor of anthologies for younger children as well as high-school pupils. She is even better known as translator of numerous children's books, and her thorough-going knowledge of folklore and fairy tales has stood her in good stead in the many projects she has undertaken for South African publishers.

Phyllis Savory was born in 1901 on a farm in what was then Southern Rhodesia and is now Zimbabwe. As child she listened with her playmates to the stories told around the evening fires – the start of a life-long passion for African folklore. During her sojourns in various countries in Africa she collected many stories, concentrating specifically on stories about the hare. She only started writing at the age of sixty – and then published nineteen volumes of stories in the space of thirty years!

Hugh Tracey was born in England in 1903 and came to what is now Zimbabwe as a young man of eighteen, to farm. He learned the local language, Karanga (one of the dialects of Shona), and was amazed to discover what a wealth of music there was amongst the local populace. He made it his life's work to record, preserve and propagate the music and folklore of Southern and Central Africa. In 1954 he founded the International Library of African Music, which falls under the auspices of Rhodes University in Grahamstown.

Annari van der Merwe was children's book editor at Tafelberg Publishers before starting up Kwela Books, a publisher specialising in publications coming from previously disadvantaged communities. She has written a volume of children's verse, as well as various articles and photo-articles in magazines.

Cicely van Straten was born in Alice in the Eastern Cape but grew up in Kenya and Uganda – hence her countless stories with an East African background. She has a Master's degree in Folklore and her long and very successful career as a writer began with her writing stories for her own children.

With numerous volumes of poetry and short stories to his name, as well as dramas, novels and children's books, **George Weideman** is one of the most versatile Afrikaans authors, and his work has been awarded numerous prizes. After a long career as a lecturer in Afrikaans he is now writing full-time.

About the Artists

"Baba Afrika" is a nom de plume.

Neels Britz was born in Pretoria in 1977 and attended the Pro Arte Alphen Park High School, where he obtained a distinction in Painting and Printmaking. He studied animation and computer graphics at the Rand Afrikaans University, receiving a Diploma in Media Studies. He has exhibited at studio exhibitions and his animated films have been shown at the Ottawa Animation Festival in Canada and on South African television. His favoured medium is pencil on paper.

Jonathan Comerford was born in Cape Town in 1961. He obtained a Diploma in Fine Art from the Frank Joubert Art School and studied printmaking at Peacock Printmaking Studio and Cyrenian Art Centre in Aberdeen, Scotland. In 1988 he set up Hardground Printmaker's Workshop in Cape Town. He has held several solo exhibitions and participated in a number of group exhibitions both locally and abroad, and his work is represented in public and corporate collections.

"Nikolaas de Kat" is a nom de plume.

Jean Fullalove was born in Lydenburg in 1927. She studied commercial art at the Michaelis Art School of the University of Cape Town and spent twenty years doing fashion drawing for newspapers and magazines. She has received awards for her animation videos for children, which have all appeared in serial form on television. She has illustrated many educational readers and textbooks and enjoys working in gouache.

Lyn Gilbert was born in Durban in 1942. She graduated with a BA in Fine Art from the University of Natal and a Master of Fine Art from Rhodes University. Lyn has held various exhibitions of her oil paintings, many of which hang in private collections both nationally and internationally. She has illustrated a large number of children's books, both for the trade and for educational publishers, locally as well as abroad.

Diek Grobler was born in Warmbaths in 1961. He obtained a BA in Fine Art from Pretoria University and an MA in Fine Art from the University of the Witwatersrand. He has had ten international solo and two-person shows and six group exhibitions and has received awards for sculpture, painting and performance art. His work hangs in various public and corporate collections both in South Africa and in Europe. Diek favours any medium that suits the work in hand.

Piet Grobler was born in Nylstroom in 1959. He has a BA and BD in Theology from the University of Pretoria, a B Honours in Journalism from the University of Stellenbosch and a Diploma in Graphic Design from the Cape Town Technical College. Piet has had many solo, two-person and group exhibitions of both paintings and illustrations. He has received a number of awards, both in South Africa and abroad. He is currently reading for an MA in Fine Art in Illustration.

Jo Harvey was born in 1964 in Cape Town. She obtained a BA Fine Art Honours Degree in Illustration and Art History from the University of Stellenbosch. She has exhibited works at the Infin Art Gallery in Cape Town and at the Bologna Children's Book Fair in Italy and has illustrated both trade and educational books for young children. She is currently studying for an MA in English literature and writing a novel.

Marna Hattingh was born in Bloemfontein in 1977. She studied fine art at the University of Stellenbosch and obtained a BAFA Honours Degree in Illustration. Marna has exhibited her work in Cape Town and in Stellenbosch. After her studies she travelled abroad for some time before returning to Cape Town, where she is engaged in illustrating her third picture book.

Robert Hichens was born in Durban in 1962. He studied graphic design at the Cape Technicon and spent twelve years in the clothing industry as a designer. He has freelanced as an illustrator of educational books since 2000 and paints in his spare time. His watercolour paintings are sold in galleries abroad.

Natalie Hinrichsen was born in Cape Town in 1974. She obtained a Diploma in Graphic Design from the Cape Technicon, majoring in Illustration and Graphic Design. She has done spot illustrations for magazines, advertising storyboards and website icons and has exhibited her work at the Infin Art Gallery in Cape Town. Natalie has illustrated many school readers and textbooks as well as picture books for the trade. Her preferred medium is gouache.

Tamsin Hinrichsen was born in Cape Town in 1974. She obtained a Diploma in Graphic Design from the Cape Technikon, majoring in Illustration and Graphic Design. She received a gold medal at the Student Loeries and has exhibited her work at the Infin Art Gallery in Cape Town. Tamsin has illustrated many educational school readers and textbooks, as well as picture books for the trade. Her preferred medium is acrylic.

Nicolaas Maritz was born in 1959 in Pretoria. He obtained a BA Honours in Fine Art from the University of Cape Town and has held over forty solo exhibitions as well as group exhibitions both locally and abroad. He has also illustrated a number of children's books and has received international prizes for his work. Nicolaas is a full-time professional artist and works in mixed media, but prefers enamel paint on hardboard for most paintings and illustrations.

Padraic O'Meara was born in Cape Town in 1980. He studied traditional cel and computer animation at the City Varsity Film and Television School, obtaining a Diploma in Animation for Film and Television. He has subsequently worked on various 2d and 3d projects and is currently working on illustrations for a children's book that he has written. Padraic favours watercolour for traditional illustration and manipulates scanned pen and ink images on computer.

Véronique Tadjo was born in Paris in 1955. She studied at the Université Nationale of the Ivory Coast and at the Sorbonne in Paris and was awarded a Fullbright Scholarship to Howard University in Washington DC, where she studied English and African American Civilization and Culture. She obtained a *Licence*, a *Maîtrise* and a PhD from these institutions respectively. She has exhibited her paintings internationally and writes and illustrates children's books.

Geoffrey Walton was born in Cape Town in 1972. He obtained a Diploma in Graphic Design from the Ruth Prowse School of Art. He has illustrated many educational readers and textbooks and is currently employed by the Council for Scientific and Industrial Research as a web page designer. Geoff enjoys working with pen and ink. He scans these images to computer where he manipulates and colours them.

Teresa Williams was born in Cape Town in 1962 and received a Bachelor of Fine Art (Honours) degree from Rhodes University. She is a book designer and cover illustrator and teaches oil painting. Her preferred medium is oil paint.

Judy Woodborne was born in Cape Town in 1966 and obtained BAFA and Master of Fine Art degrees from the University of Cape Town. She has held several solo exhibitions and participated in numerous group exhibitions and print biennales both locally and abroad. Her work is represented in public and corporate art collections internationally, including those of the Smithsonian Institute and the Musée d'Art Contemporain of Chamalières, France. She continues to pursue her printmaking interests.

Acknowledgements

"The Enchanting Song of the Magical Bird" was first published in *From the Heart of the Fire* by Julius Oelke. Tafelberg, Cape Town, 1995. □ "The Cat Who Came Indoors", "Kamiyo of the River" and "Sakunaka, the Handsome Young Man" were first published in *The Lion on the Path* by Hugh Tracey. Routledge & Kegan Paul, New York, 1967. □ "The Great Thirst", "King Lion's Gifts" and "Wolf and Jackal and the Barrel of Butter" were originally published in Afrikaans in *Die Mooiste Afrikaanse Sprokies* by Pieter W. Grobbelaar. Human & Rousseau, Cape Town, 1968. □ "The Message" by George Weideman was originally published in Afrikaans in *Goue Fluit, my Storie is Uit*, compiled by Linda Rode. Tafelberg, Cape Town, 1988. □ "The Snake Chief" and "The Guardian of the Pool" were first published in *Catch Me a River* by Diana Pitcher. Tafelberg, Cape Town, 1990. □ "How Hlakanyana Outwitted the Monster" was first published in *Tales of the Trickster Boy* by Jack Cope. Tafelberg, Cape Town, 1990. □ "Words As Sweet As Honey from Sankhambi", previously unpublished, is a translation of the Afrikaans retelling by Linda Rode of an old Venda story. □ "Mmutla and Phiri", "The Lion, the Hare and the Hyena", "The Hare and the Tree Spirit", "The Hare's Revenge" and "The Cloud Princess" were first published in *The Little Wise One* by Phyllis Savory. Tafelberg, Cape Town, 1990. □ "Mmadipetsane" was originally published in Afrikaans in *As die Maan oor die Lug Loop* by Minnie Postma. Tafelberg, Cape Town, 1986. □ "Spider and the Crows" is a translation of the Afrikaans tale in *Husse Met Ore*, Tafelberg, Cape Town, 1993. It was originally published in German in a collection of folk tales entitled *Als die Baüme in den Himmel Wuchsen* by Eugen Diederichs Verlag, Düsseldorf/Cologne, 1977. □ "Natiki" was originally published in Afrikaans in *Die Kalbasdraertjie* by Glaudien Kotzé. Tafelberg, Cape Town, 1987. □ "The Mantis and the Moon" was first published in *The Mantis and the Moon* by Marguerite Poland. Ravan Press, Johannesburg, 1979. □ "The Snake with Seven Heads" is a revised version of the original picture book by Gcina Mhlophe. Skotaville, Braamfontein, 1989. □ "The Wolf Queen" and "The Sultan's Daughter" were originally published in Afrikaans in *Doederomandro en Ander Kaapse Stories* by I. D. du Plessis. Human & Rousseau, Cape Town, 1970. □ "Van Hunks and the Devil" by Annari van der Merwe was originally published in Afrikaans in *Goue Lint, my Storie Begint*, compiled by Linda Rode. Tafelberg, Cape Town, 1985. □ "The Ring of the King" by Jay Heale was first published in *Storytime*, compiled by the author. Tafelberg, Cape Town, 1987. □ "The Clever Snake Charmer" was originally published in Afrikaans in *Kinders van die Wêreld*, Volume 5, compiled by C. F. Albertyn and J. J. Spies. Albertyn, Cape Town, 1963. □ "Asmodeus and the Bottler of Djinns" was first published in *Asmodeus – A Forkful of Tales from Devil's Peak* by Alex D'Angelo. Tafelberg, Cape Town, 1997. □ "The Mother Who Turned to Dust" by Kasiya Makaka Phiri is published here for the first time. □ "Mpipidi and the Motlopi Tree" was first published in *Stories South of the Sun*, compiled by Linda Rode and Hans and Christel Bodenstein. Tafelberg, Cape Town, 1993. □ "Fesito Goes to Market" by Cicely van Straten was first published in *The Great Snake of Kalungu and Other East African Stories*. Juventus, Pretoria, 1981. □ "Sannie Langtand and the Visitor" was first published in *The Trouble with Sannie Langtand* by Alex D'Angelo. Tafelberg, Cape Town, 1997.